Blood & Bones

Peter Tabern

Illustrated by Korky Paul

Andersen Press · London

For Daniel and David (K.P. – illustrator)

First published in 1995 by
Andersen Press Limited,
20 Vauxhall Bridge Road, London SW1V 2SA

British Library Cataloguing in Publication Data is available
ISBN 0-86264-621-9

Typesetting by The Harrington Consultancy Ltd., London N1
Printed and bound in Great Britain by
the Guernsey Press Company Limited, Guernsey, Channel Islands

The Childsplay Production of PIRATES for BBC Television is produced
and directed by Peter Tabern, executive producer, Albert Barber, and scripts
by Rebecca Stevens and Peter Tabern.

Where's Spot? © Eric Hill, 1980. Extract appears by permission of
Ventura Publishing Limited

Contents

Introduction

It was night. It was the dead of night. In fact it was the softly dripping, gently oozing, 'Who-left-that-there?', 'Oh-blast-I-think-I've-stepped-in-it!', blob of nastiness in the gutter of the night, when Blind Pew came tap-tapping down Wordsworth Close and stopped outside the Pirates' front door.

Gran was going to be eighty-four tomorrow and to celebrate she had gone straight to hammock without any supper. (This was to leave room for all the birthday cake she planned to eat the following day.) But then at the last minute she felt so hungry she just had to have that piece of blue cheese from the back of the poultice cupboard washed down with the tiniest drop of rum.

And now, as if to punish her, here was old Pew a-banging on her door fit to wake the dead. Poor old Gran. Without wanting to, she found herself creeping down the hall and slowly opening the front door.

'Yes?' she said and gave herself a shock because her voice had gone all echoey. 'What is it?' The figure on the doorstep wore a huge black cloak with a hood so deep and dark you could have jumped inside and vanished for ever and when he spoke his voice was like bat-claws scratching on a graveyard wall.

5

'Abigail Blood, do you know who I am?' He raised his stick at Gran and though her knees turned to thin grey gruel, she had the sense to play for time.

'Have you come to rod the drains?' she asked. 'Only it's a bit late and...' The figure drew itself up to its full height and hissed.

'They call me...Blind Pew.'

Of course Gran had known who it was all along but she pretended to be surprised.

'Not...not the Blind Pew who according to legend visits each and every Pirate on the eve of their death?' Pew was always pleased to be recognised.

'The very same.'

'Never heard of you,' she said and tried to shut the door but the horror was too quick for her.

'Abigail Blood, stay where you are!' His voice made the gruel drain out of her knees and collect in a puddle round her ankles. 'Abigail Blood, your time is up and I am sent to summon you.' Although Pew did not strike Gran as the sympathetic type, she decided to appeal to his better nature and began to snivel pathetically.

'What do you want with me? I'm just a helpless old woman. I'm eighty-four tomorrow, you know...'

'Exactly!' said Pew and when he leaned towards her his wheezy breath smelled of bladderwrack and old sea boots. 'Abigail Blood, your days are numbered and the number is very small.' Gran

stopped snivelling and eyed him cautiously.

'How small?' Pew held up one long, bony finger and waved it under her nose.

'Aargh!' Her eyes crossed and she started to cry. 'It's not fair! What about my birthday?'

'I'm sorry, I can't help that,' said Pew, 'I just do summonses. So don't make a fuss and hold out your hand.' Gran almost fell for it. She started to do as she was told but at the last moment something stopped her. She drew back and her eyes narrowed craftily.

'Oh no you don't. I know your game.' It had been a long time since she'd heard this story but there are some things a Pirate never forgets. Yes, it was all coming back to her. 'You're trying to give me the Black Spot, aren't you? I remember now. And if I take it I'll be doomed, won't I?' Pew looked decidedly shifty.

'Er…no, not necessarily…'

'Hah! So you may say, matey, so you may say!' Gran was getting her confidence back. 'Well I'm not going to take it and you can't make me!' Pew sighed.

'Look,' he said, trying to sound friendly, 'it's not the Black Spot, it's something else. Something nice.' Why did he always get the awkward ones last thing at night? 'Now, come on, just hold out your hand…please.' But Gran was having none of it.

'No! I don't want to be summoned! I don't want to be doomed! I want my birthday! I want prezzies and cake!' When Pew heard this he started to laugh, not a happy sound, more like coffin nails rattling in a dead man's chest.

'Prezzies and cake? Prezzies and cake? What *are* you talking about? You're rotten to your family, vile to the neighbours and a complete stranger to soap and water. Who'd be giving you prezzies, eh?' Now Gran *knew* she was getting a cake (mainly because she had baked it herself) but come to think of it, who *would* be giving her prezzies?

'That's right.' Pew leaned closer than ever. 'No one. No one exceptin' old Blind Pew. Now, *hold out your hand!*' The puddle of gruel froze round Gran's feet, sticking her firmly to the doorstep, and as Pew reached forward, holding something in his outstretched hand, all she could do was close her eyes very tightly and wail in despair…

'No, no, noooo…'

1
Prezzies and Pan Scrape

'Hold out your hand!' Lambkin Bones shook Gran by the shoulder and Roger drew back the curtains, letting the daylight flood into the Pirates' living room. Ever since they had been ashore they had tried to get Gran to sleep upstairs, preferably in a bed, but it was no good. In all the time they had been in Wordsworth Close she had only ventured upstairs once, and that was when she mistook poor Mr Jones for her old dancing partner the Beast of Bangalore, and made him walk the plank out of the bedroom window. Gran did not believe in stairs or beds or houses for that matter, so she slung her hammock from the living-room ceiling, beneath the bowsprit of her last ship, *The Smoking Beagle*.

Now she burrowed deep under the covers and wondered why Blind Pew's voice had suddenly gone all high but she had no intention of coming up to find out.

'Hold out your hand!' said Lambkin again.

'Eighty-four today, eighty-four today,' sang Roger merrily. 'Prezzie time!' and as Man-in-the-Sack arrived with her breakfast tray, Roger flung back the covers.

'Aargh!' Gran let out a yell and sat bolt upright. Without her teeth and with her hair full of curlers made from the bones of small dead animals, Gran was always a bit of a shock first thing but *this* particular morning she looked especially hideous. Roger was shocked.

'Mother-in-Law, what on earth's the matter? You look as if you've seen a ghost.'

'Worse, far worse! I've seen Blind Pew his very self!' Of course nobody believed her. Even Baby, doing push-ups in his big black pram, stopped to laugh and Man-in-the-Sack wagged a warning finger. Gran had obviously been having one of her cheesy dreams.

'What was it this time, Gran?' asked Lambkin. 'Not that old piece of Gorgonzola?'

'Washed down with a nip of grog, I'll be bound.' In Roger's experience late night snacks always gave old people bad dreams although rum and blue cheese tended to produce dreams of great white sharks and horrible ends in far-flung places, which were just the sort of dreams Gran usually liked.

'Don't you look sideways at me, Roger Bones.' Gran had caught Roger smirking. 'Tried to give me the Black Spot he did, but I wouldn't take it. Not me, not Abigail Blood. I was too clever for him.'

'Nonsense, Mother-in-Law, it was just a dream. Now sit up and have some breakfast.'

'It's your favourite,' said Lambkin, taking the mug and spoon from the tray. 'Pan scrape and Lucozade. It'll settle your stomach.' She gave the mug a quick stir to stop the skin getting any thicker.

'I don't want my stomach settled. I want to know if that old devil Pew's a-lurkin' and a-skulkin' outside.'

'Of course he isn't,' said Roger. 'And really, Mother-in-Law, when Man-in-the-Sack's gone to the trouble of making you a birthday breakfast, I think the least you can do is drink it before it sets.' But Gran clamped her mouth tight shut and shook her head till her curlers rattled. Roger decided not to argue, after all it was the old bat's birthday. 'Very well then, what about your prezzies? Just look at these…' The postman had brought seven bottle-shaped parcels, goodwill messages from Gran's Pirate chums, and Man-in-the-Sack had arranged them in a neat row on the table. 'What a lucky birthday girl she is! Don't you want to open them?'

'Not me, matey.' Gran rolled her eyes. 'I'm not touching 'em! Any one of them might have the Black Spot inside. One squint and I'd be doomed…'

Of course Lambkin knew about Blind Pew and the Black Spot, all Pirates did. Even the land-crabs knew because of *Treasure Island*. But she also knew it was just a legend. Not even Gran could believe there actually *was* a guy in a cloak somewhere who went around handing out Black Spots.

'Come on, Gran, you can't really believe all that old rubbish. Tell her. She can't, can she, Dad?'

'Well, you know, it's a funny thing,' said Roger

thoughtfully, 'I've seen old Pirates right as ninepence one minute, they get the Black Spot and poof! Out like a light...' He clicked his fingers. 'Just like that. Off to the Great Crow's Nest in the sky. *Adios, compadre...*' Gran's eyes rolled in earnest, further and further until only the yellows were showing, then she gave a long groan and fell back into the hammock. Roger smiled. 'Yes, people in far better shape than old Misery Guts to be honest...'

'Thanks Dad, thanks a lot. That's just what she needed.' Lambkin was furious. How could he do it? It was as if he *wanted* Gran to be all depressed on her birthday. She clambered up on a sea-chest so she could lean over the hammock. 'Don't listen to him, Gran, he doesn't know what he's talking about. I mean, come on, how scary can a "Black Spot" be?' Gran did not answer, she just put her head under the covers and groaned piteously. 'What does it look like, this Black Spot? Sort of drawn on a bit of paper is it, Gran? Coloured in with felt tip or biro or something?' Gran poked her head out.

'How do I know? I haven't seen it. I wouldn't be here if I'd seen it, would I? I'd be dead, you stupid girl...' and she disappeared again. Roger sniggered and Lambkin glared at him as she snatched up a paper and pencil from the table.

'Okay, okay, you've never seen it. Right. So what's to stop anyone doing it? What's to stop me? I could just go round drawing black spots on bits of paper

13

and handing them out to people I don't like.' And she tore off the corner of the paper, drew a rough black blob and waved it in front of the hammock. 'There you go. Easy.'

Without thinking, Gran lifted the covers to have a quick squint, saw the Black Spot right in front of her nose and let out a roar fit to wake the Dead Druids' Display Team.

'Aargh!' she screamed. 'I'm doomed! Doomed! My own granddaughter's a-scribblin' Black Spots! Any minute now the Dark Dealer in Death will come knocking at that door!' And sure enough, as the Pirates followed her trembling hand, there was a loud knock on the living-room door. Everyone froze. Even Baby froze. Even Pustule, Gran's foul-mouthed macaw, froze in mid-scratch, his foot stuck stupidly in his ear. Only Gran, who had spent quite enough time being frozen recently, sprang to life. She hurled herself backwards out of the hammock, bounced off an old powder keg and landed with a sickening thud as the door swung open to reveal... Lawrence Kitten, Lambkin's friend from next door. He was carrying a nicely wrapped birthday present and stood in the doorway blinking and pushing his glasses up his nose, something he did quite often when he was puzzled.

'Sorry,' he said. 'You didn't hear me and the door was open...'

'What a relief,' said Roger. 'We thought you

might be…never mind. Look, Mother-in-Law, here's young Lawrence with a present for you…Mother-in-Law?'

Gran appeared suddenly from behind a treasure chest, struggling to cock her enormous brass blunderbuss.

'Sneak up on a girl's blind side, would you?' she yelled. 'I'll teach you, you worm-sucking grave-licker!' Before she could take proper aim, she tripped on the hem of her nightie and fired wildly across the room. The force of the explosion knocked her flat and the room filled with so much smoke it was a while before the others could see that Lawrence was quite unhurt (although the stuffed iguana above the door would never roller skate again). Keen to get another shot in, Gran had swapped the blunderbuss for her flintlock pistols.

'Stand and take it like a man!' she screamed at no one in particular. 'Abigail Blood doesn't go down without a fight!' But having said that, she promptly went down like a ton of bricks as Man-in-the-Sack and Roger hurled themselves across the room and wrestled her to the ground.

2
A Birthday Surprise

'She shot at Lawrence!' Lawrence's mum was understandably concerned. Roger sipped his second cup of coffee and helped himself to a fig roll.

'Yes, and missed by a mile. So you can tell she's upset.' They were sitting in Helen Kitten's kitchen which was probably Roger's favourite place in the world. For one thing it was clean and usually smelled of something nice that had just been cooked, and for another it never had his mother-in-law in it, which to Roger's mind made it just about perfect.

Roger and Helen were friends. In fact since he had moved the family ashore, Helen was the only real friend Roger had made among the shore folk, the 'land-crabs' as Gran called them. Helen had dark wavy hair and brown eyes that sparkled when she was happy and flashed when she was upset, and she got upset when old Pirates took pot-shots at Lawrence.

'What's the matter with her?' she asked. 'I thought she was looking forward to her birthday.'

'She was, she was,' agreed Roger, 'but then Blind Pew visited her in a dream and tried to give her the Black Spot. Now she thinks everybody's out to kill her.'

'You can't be serious,' said Helen. 'Blind Pew?

Like in the book?'

'Oh yes, absolutely,' said Roger. Helen always tried to see the other person's point of view but it was hard to picture a minor character from *Treasure Island* ruining your birthday. 'It's very depressing for a Pirate to get the Black Spot,' Roger went on, 'it means you're going to drop dead within twenty-four hours.' Helen tried to get into the spirit of it.

'Yes, well, I can see how that would be depressing. Er, what exactly does it look like, this Black Spot?' Roger looked blank.

'Sorry, Helen, haven't a clue. You see she hasn't actually *got* it, not as such. That's the point. But she can't leave the house and she can't take anything from anybody, just in case the Black Spot's hidden inside.'

'Can't be easy on your birthday, with everyone giving you presents,' said Helen, beginning to get the hang of it. 'Poor Mrs Blood, she must be having a terrible time.'

'Yes,' said Roger, smiling happily and reaching for another biscuit, 'she is.'

Over at the Pirates' house, Gran had been persuaded to sit at the table and had even toyed with her pan scrape and Lucozade. The family had bought her the very latest side-handled police baton, which at any other time would have had her jumping for joy. Today it did not even raise a smile and on no account would she touch the presents from her old shipmates.

In the end Lambkin and Lawrence decided to open them for her. Not surprisingly, they all contained bottles, some of which were filled with rum and some of which were filled with other things. Lawrence came across one filled with a murky greenish liquid in which something had been pickled, although even after he had cleaned his glasses twice he could not make out what it was. There was a card stuck to the neck of the bottle with a big blob of sealing wax. Lambkin carefully broke the seal and spread out the message.

'It's from Vilespleen the Heartless. It says, "Good luck on your eighty-fourth and a big thumbs-up from all the lads down the Whistling Leper."'

'What's in the bottle?' asked Lawrence giving the pickled thing a shake.

'A big thumb,' said Lambkin and sure enough, it was. 'That's nice isn't it, Gran? Makes it sort of personal…'

'Don't you bring it near me!' said Gran, terrified that the cursed spot might be swimming around in there with Vilespleen's pickled digit. Lambkin sighed.

'Well how about this one?' She held up a bright blue bottle on which the sender had painted a big pink rose. Although there was no message, there was a heavy marlin spike fastened to the cork and

Lambkin immediately used it to smash the bottle, which Lawrence now realised was just a sort of Pirate envelope.

'Oh Gran, look.' Lambkin carefully fished out a rolled-up photograph from among the broken glass. 'It's from Grog Blossom Kate. It says, "Happy Birthday, Squitter-Head. If looking in the mirror depresses you, why not stick a picture of someone younger over the top." And she's sent you a picture of herself.'

'The cheeky madam!' Grog Blossom Kate was Gran's oldest friend, eighty-four if she was a day. 'Has she still got hairy nostrils?' asked Gran, trying to stop herself peeping at the photograph. Lambkin stared closely.

'I think so. It's hard to tell with the moustache.' Gran almost looked but then shook her head so violently her false teeth clattered.

'No! Get thee behind me Satan, and don't push!' She would have liked nothing better than to see what the years had done to old Kate but then any one of the woman's hideous moles and obscene warts might be hiding the Black Spot. It was just too risky. Lawrence meanwhile was trying to make sense of the picture.

'What's she doing with a sink plunger in her mouth?' Lambkin had a closer look.

'That's not a sink plunger, that's her mouth. Look, she's got a pistol in it.' Gran began to laugh.

'Ah, yes. That's Kate all right. Never went anywhere without her pistol. "The sharp shooter with the hairy hooter" we used to call her.' Lawrence was staring hard but could still only see a sink plunger. Gran's voice had gone all dreamy and far-away. 'Great days, great days,' she murmured to herself and dabbed her eyes with a corner of the tablecloth. Lambkin put her hand gently on the old woman's arm and Gran suddenly seemed to remember where she was. 'Here, girl, what about our Molly? Is there one from your mother?' Lambkin's face became serious.

'I haven't seen one but why don't you have a look? There's still a couple we haven't opened. Come on, Gran, you know you want to.' But it was no use.

'Not me, matey. You never know from what quarter the Grim Harbinger of Doom will strike.' Then Lawrence had an idea. Surely there was nothing to stop Mrs Blood opening *his* present? Lambkin thought about it.

'Why not? Lawrence isn't the Harbinger of Doom. I mean look at him, he's not even particularly Grim.' Lawrence pushed his glasses up his nose and held out his neatly wrapped gift. Gran wavered. Her fingers were itching to get hold of a prezzie, any prezzie, even a funny looking square one from a land-crab. Her hands made sort of spidery movements in mid-air then all at once she snatched the present and began tearing frantically at the paper. Man-in-the-Sack clapped and so did the children until they realised that Gran had gone very quiet and was staring suspiciously at the opened present.

'Well,' said Lambkin. 'Say "Thank you" to Lawrence.'

'What is it?' said Gran suspiciously. She was holding a grey plastic box with a small square screen and a few black buttons.

'It's called a Game Boy,' said Lawrence. 'You play it, watch.' He took hold of the box and pressed one or two of its buttons, whereupon a chirruping, bleeping sound filled the room and what looked to Gran like an army of Black Spots began to scurry on the tiny screen.

Her eyes widened in horror and she let out a roar.

'Aargh! I'll kill the Game Boy! I'll pull out its teeth and use them for tiddly-winks!' She drew her side-handled baton. 'Find me its mouth, boy, find me its mouth!' And before anyone could stop her she swung the baton and began to thrash the unfortunate machine to within an inch of its miserable life.

When Lawrence got home, Roger Bones and Helen were still in the kitchen.

'Well?' said Helen. 'Did Mrs Blood like her present?'

'Not exactly,' said Lawrence. Helen looked disappointed.

'We got her a Game Boy,' she explained to Roger. 'Actually it was my idea.'

'Mm, nice,' said Roger politely although it seemed an odd sort of choice for an eighty-four year-old.

'Anyway,' said Lawrence, 'I'm pretty sure she'd never seen one before.'

'Strange,' said Roger. 'She's had lots of Cabin Boys. They must be similar surely?' Helen tried to put him right.

'No, Roger, you don't understand. The Game Boy is electronic with several levels of difficulty.'

'Well, just so long as he doesn't burn the toast, eh Lawrence, or he'll be over the side with no difficulty at all.' Helen thought about trying to explain but did not really know where to begin.

'Look,' she said at last, 'maybe you should all get out a bit more. Let's think of somewhere we could take Mrs Blood.' Roger thought of a good place but was not sure his mother-in-law would be allowed down a disused coal mine. 'Come on, Roger, what does Mrs Blood like doing more than anything else?' This was a tricky one. Roger could only think of drinking and shouting, and even when Lawrence helpfully added belching, it was obvious Helen thought they weren't really trying.

'I know,' she said, 'we could all take her out for a

special birthday meal. How about it, Lawrence? We could take her to Plato's.' Roger was horrified.

'You want Mother-in-Law to eat something? In public? Are you mad?'

'No, it's brilliant, Mr Bones,' said Lawrence. 'It's called the Greek Funspot. They've got singing and plate smashing and sparklers in the pudding. It's great. Mrs Blood will love it.' Roger doubted that very much but at the same time he was not exactly looking forward to an evening at home playing Dodge the Spot.

'How was she when you left, Lawrence? Did she seem pretty lively?'

'Definitely.' Gran's flailing baton was still quite fresh in his mind. 'Man-in-the-Sack was singing to her.' Helen was surprised. So far as she knew, Man-in-the-Sack had never uttered a word.

'I didn't know he could sing,' said Helen.

'He can't,' said Roger grimly.

Back in the old days, the very old days before Red Eye the Wrongdoer had stuffed him in a sack and left him on a desert island, Man-in-the-Sack had been a great talker, able to bang on for hours on any topic you cared to throw at him. But by the time Roger came across him he had spent two hundred and seventeen days talking to himself and was so tired of the sound of his own voice that he never spoke again.

Unfortunately that did not stop him singing, which he did at the drop of a hat in a voice that sounded as though it had been locked away for a hundred years in a dusty cupboard. Gran liked his voice and said it reminded her of cheese, she also liked him to play the squeeze-box and thought his music was 'timeless'. Lambkin agreed and thought it was tuneless and hopeless as well.

For Gran's birthday he had come up with a special version of 'Dance Around In Your Bones'. It went like this:

'When the Captain's got the squitters
And the Bosun's belly groans
'T'ain't no sin to take off your skin
And dance around in your bones.'

As Roger came in Gran was just asking for another chorus which meant she was probably in a good mood so he waved for silence and pulled up a chair.

'So, how's the birthday girl?' Gran grunted and knocked her pipe out on the side of the sugar bowl. 'Lots of nice prezzies I see.'

'If you say so, matey,' said Gran. 'I'm not touching them.' Roger took a deep breath and pressed on.

'How would you feel, later say, about going out for a bite to eat?' Gran gave him the look she saved for rum bottles which turned out to be unexpectedly empty.

'Roger Bones, I have sat here all day, a prisoner on my own ship, trying to avoid the dreaded Spot. Frankly I need to go out like I need three dalmatians and a dose of chicken pox.'

'I take it that's a "no" then,' said Roger. The side-handled baton slammed down on the table-top and she grabbed him by the shirt front.

'Watch my lips, matey. Nothing would get me through that door today, not if you was to tie me to a ten-foot pole and fill my mouth with rancid football socks. Is that quite clear?'

Later that evening a taxi drew up in Wordsworth Close and a strange procession could be seen leaving the Boneses' house. First came Helen and Lawrence and bringing up the rear was Lambkin. But in the middle, wrapped in a cargo net and slung from a ten-foot pole carried by Roger and Man-in-the-Sack, was Gran. She was squirming and writhing and her terrible oaths would certainly have taken the paint off the front door and brought out every land-crab in the street had not her mouth been stuffed full of blue and white football socks.

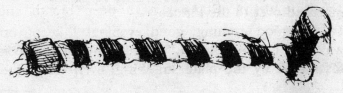

3
Plato Potatos and the Greek Funspot

The Greek Funspot was a friendly sort of place with loud folk music, twinkling coloured lights and lots of candles in bottles. The owner, Plato, was short and round and wore a lot of gold jewellery which jingled when he walked and jangled when he danced around doing Greek plate smashing, which is what he was up to when the Pirates arrived.

His assistant, Spiros, showed the Pirates to a table and once they had unwrapped Gran and tied her securely to a chair, they settled down to watch the floor show.

There was only one other table occupied, by a fat woman, a thin man and two sour-faced children. Plato was giving it everything he had got to keep them entertained, leaping around wildly, flinging china in all directions, and shaking his fingers under the noses of the children in what Lambkin supposed was a traditional form of greeting.

After a while the music stopped and with a final flourish Plato sent a large dinner plate crashing into the corner above the thin man's head. Then he turned sharply on his heel, straightened his tie and marched over to the Pirates.

'Ah, good evening, good evening! I keep you waiting, I hate myself.' The Pirates had been fascinated by the plate smashing, even Gran had

28

stopped struggling, and they had not minded waiting in the least.

'Don't mention it, my dear chap,' said Roger untying Gran's menu hand. 'We were just admiring your folk dancing.' Plato looked blank.

'Eh?...Oh no, kind sir, is not folk dancing, is final warning. Naughty kiddies don't eat their moussaka...' and he picked up Roger's side plate and frisbeed it at the head of the sour-faced girl. 'So, I am Plato Potatos, this is my restaurant and you are welcome to it.' He smiled a gold-toothed smile which became much wider when he caught sight of Helen. 'Ah, Missis Kitten, is adorable to see you...' and he took her hand and began kissing it loudly. Lambkin and Lawrence looked at each other and Lawrence put his fingers down his throat and made going-to-be-sick noises. Lambkin giggled and Helen glared at them but Plato didn't seem to notice, he just carried on kissing. In the end Roger thought someone ought to say something.

'Er... I've always been a great admirer of your country, Mr Potatos. All those olive groves and bits of old temple lying about. Marvellous.' By this time Plato had reached Helen's elbow.

'I wouldn't know, sir, I come from Leigh-on-Sea,' and he would have gone on towards her shoulder but Helen eased her arm away.

'Actually, Plato, if you remember this is rather a special occasion.' She pointed towards Gran.

'Of course I remember,' said Plato proudly and he took from his pocket a badge saying 'I am 84' in big red letters. 'Today is the Happy Birthday of Missis Pirate. This I know, and believe me she will have one Funspot night to remember!' He began to fasten the badge on Gran's frock coat. 'Oh yes, the singing, the dancing, the sparklers in the pud!'

All the time his voice was getting louder and louder as if he were talking to the deaf or at least to the hard of understanding.

'Hello, Missis Pirate!' he shouted in Gran's ear. 'Many returns to you. Are you having a jolly time today?' He was having trouble with the badge and his tie was dangerously close to Gran's face but by the time anyone noticed, it was already too late. With the speed of a striking puff-adder on its way to a good party, Gran had the poor man by the throat and it took both Roger and Man-in-the-Sack to prise her fingers loose and get her back to her chair.

Plato rubbed the red marks on his neck and Gran roared at him through a mouthful of blue and white socks. Of course when he looked closely at the socks, Plato realised why the old woman had attacked him.

'Ah, I see you are a Chelsea supporter.' He gave her his widest, goldest smile and tapped his chest proudly.

'Hey, me too! Glen Hoddle. Dennis Wise. Come on you Blues! Very good, eh?' Gran had one hand free and began tugging at the socks. If she was not allowed to hit anybody, at least she could empty her mouth and have a good swear. Roger naturally began stuffing them back as quickly as he could.

'Oh gosh,' said Plato, 'you are a very hungry old lady and I keep you waiting. I hate myself. One second only and we will find you something nicer than the rancid sockies. I will go around and come...'

'I'm sorry, Roger,' said Helen. 'Maybe this wasn't such a good idea.'

'Nonsense,' said Roger who had secretly been thinking the same thing, 'we love it, don't we, Mother-in-Law?' But Gran was already trying to steal drinks from Spiros' tray.

Lambkin meanwhile was watching the sour-faced children at the other table. The boy had finished his meal but his sister was still playing with half a plate of soggy moussaka and Plato, on his way to get the Pirates' menus, had spotted her. 'Oh good,' thought Lambkin. 'More flying crockery.' But this time Plato simply picked up the girl's moussaka and without a word tipped it on her head before handing the empty plate to her mother.

'If she wants anything else,' he said calmly, 'tell her to snap her fingers...one at a time.' And with that he marched off to the kitchen.

Lambkin had never been to a restaurant before, Greek or otherwise, but if this was the way land-crabs behaved you obviously had to choose your food with care. She watched the moussaka slowly gloop down the girl's sour face and decided she might stick to salad if she was going to end up wearing it. At that moment Plato returned with a handful of menu cards.

'Everything tonight is wonderful,' he announced, 'except what is off,' and taking care to keep at arm's length, he waved a menu at Gran. 'So it is the Happy Birthday girl to go first. Now, hold out your hand...'

Everything went quiet. Gran knew she had heard those words somewhere before, but could not for the life of her remember where. Then she found herself looking down at the menu. All the dishes were listed in two long columns and in the middle were the words 'Greek Funspot – Eat Till You Die' printed in white – on a huge *black spot*.

'Aargh!' All the colour drained from her nose. 'The Black Spot! The Black Spot!' Plato was busy leafing through his order pad.

'I think is off,' he said absentmindedly, 'but the sheftalia is very nice...'

'I know you!' said Gran hurling the menu aside and tearing herself free. 'Hold out your hand indeed! You're him, you're Blind Pew!' Suddenly she had her side-handled baton in one hand and Plato in the other and she shook him till his jewellery jangled.

Roger was furious. All the Pirates knew his views

on carrying weapons in public and he distinctly remembered asking Man-in-the-Sack to search Gran thoroughly before the taxi arrived. Something would have to be said but in the meantime Plato's feet were barely touching the floor and his voice had gone all squeaky.

'Missis Pirate, you are making a terrible mistake. Is not Blind Poo! It is I, Plato Potatos! Ow! You are a very strong old lady!' Gran hoisted him clear of the floor.

'You'd better believe it, matey,' she snarled. 'Try to give me the Black Spot, would you?' Plato looked around desperately.

'No, no, dear madam. You got it all backwards. Is not Black Spot, is Funspot! Ha, ha, ha!' He had no idea what the crazy old aubergine was talking about but the only thing to do was humour her until help arrived. Roger knew things had gone way beyond 'humouring' and as for 'help'... He took off his jacket; if you wanted anything doing round here you had to do it yourself.

'Don't you "madam" me, you bucket of hyena offal.' Gran was lining up another baton shot and Roger, approaching from behind, walked straight into her backswing and was sent flying across the room. Gran knew she had hit something but by the time she turned round to see what it was, Roger was lying across the fat woman's lap, which convinced Gran the land-crabs were up to something. Without

further ado she began to whack Plato about the shoulders as hard as she could.

'Calm yourself, Mother-in-Law,' said Roger through a mouthful of tablecloth. 'I think he's probably telling the truth.' Lambkin sprang to her feet. Had everyone gone mad? Of course Plato was telling the truth, you only had to look at him, frantically trying to crawl under the Pirates' table.

'Come on, Gran, how can he be Blind Pew? He's not even short-sighted.' Gran stopped whacking and leaned thoughtfully on her baton. You could see very little of Plato, but what there was to see did not seem particularly Pew-like.

'Well, it's a good disguise I'll grant you,' she prodded Plato cautiously with the baton, 'but it doesn't fool Abigail Blood and if I'm for the Great Crow's Nest in the Sky, I'm taking this one with me!' She swung a ferocious blow but Plato had a last card to play.

'Wait, Missis Pirate! You haven't had your special pud! Quick, Spiros!' And he waved madly at his assistant who was already lighting the sparklers on an enormous cream trifle.

'Oh Gran! See what they've brought you!' said Lambkin, pointing to the fizzing bowl but Gran took one look and let out a yell.

'Aargh! The swines have got a bomb! Save yourself, girl. Take no prisoners!' And she rained blows down on Plato's retreating bottom for all she was worth. Roger took Spiros to one side.

'You know, I rather thought she might take this the wrong way. May I?' And he took the trifle and carried it carefully across to Gran. She was reduced to kicking at Plato who could just be heard singing 'Happy Birthday' from under the table.

'Mother-in-Law?' said Roger when Gran paused for breath. 'Would you mind taking your hat off for me?' Now she was kicking someone, Gran felt a lot more relaxed and promptly handed her battered tricorn to Man-in-the-Sack. 'Thank you,' said Roger and without warning, brought the trifle bowl down as hard as he could on top of her head.

For a moment nothing happened and then, covered in cream and quite slowly at first, with the odd sparkler still twinkling festively, Gran did a little pirouette and crashed rigid to the ground.

4
Doomed

When the Pirates got home they cleaned the custard out of Gran's ears and got her straight into her hammock. The whack on the head had done no harm, it never did. In fact Roger doubted he could hit her hard enough to do any real damage, but since she was now convinced she had been given the Black Spot and was doomed to die, he would probably never find out.

Roger whistled cheerfully as he combed his hair. He was on his way to report back to Helen who had promised to get the cocoa on. Lambkin was trying to coax Gran into eating something. She had not touched anything since the pan scrape first thing and although Man-in-the-Sack had cooked her a lovely krill supper, she would not touch a bite.

'Gran,' said Lambkin, 'you've got to eat something. Dad, tell her. She won't even talk to me.' Roger stopped whistling.

'Ah, I've seen old Pirates go like this before. They give up hope, turn their faces to the wall and wait for death to take them.' He gave his hair a final pat and checked the ribbon in his pony-tail. 'Anyway, must dash. Give me a shout if she turns blue or anything.'

'He doesn't mean it, Gran,' said Lambkin as the whistling retreated down the hall. 'Some men find it difficult to express their feelings.' Gran, who had no difficulty expressing her feelings, spat in Roger's general direction then sank back and took her granddaughter's hand.

'You're a good girl, Lambkin Bones, and when I'm gone you can have my Game Boy and my second best blunderbuss.'

'Don't talk like that,' said Lambkin.

'Quaark! Silly old fool!' said Pustule rudely. Gran glared at him.

'And you can have him.' She rapped the macaw sharply on the head with her pipe. ''Cos where I'm going I shall probably get a bat.'

'Come on, Gran, you're not going anywhere. Look what Man-in-the-Sack's got for you.' He had been off searching the kitchen for delicacies to tempt the invalid and had come up with quite a selection. 'How about a Windowlene-flavour yoghurt?' Gran shook her head weakly. 'Okay, what about a nice Day-Glo Mousse or a can of Silt?' Gran turned away. These were all her favourites, if a drop of Silt would not do the trick, things really *were* bad. Just as they were running out of ideas, Man-in-the-Sack found a pork pie that looked strangely familiar. Lambkin blew the fluff off and held it up.

'Ah, I remember this. It's *yours,* Gran, see, it's got your spare set in it!' And sure enough Gran's false teeth were still clamped firmly to the crust.

'Nah,' said Gran. 'Give it to Baby.' Then she had

a better idea. 'Wait, hang on to the gnashers, I'd like Grog Blossom Kate to have them.' It was a kind thought so Lambkin prised them loose and tucked them away for safekeeping while Man-in-the-Sack took Baby off for a quick game of snooker before bed.

'You know the one thing I regret, girlie?' said Gran when they were on their own. 'Aside from leaving you and the nipper of course. I shall go to the Great Crow's Nest without clapping eyes on our Molly.' Molly was Lambkin's mum, and although she wrote to them, they had not seen her in all the time they had been living ashore. This made Lambkin miserable, but like Gran always said, her mum was a Blood, not a Bones. She could never have settled down in Wordsworth Close. That was why she and Roger had split up. Lambkin bit her lip but Gran became all watery-eyed.

'Call me old-fashioned,' she sniffed, 'but I sort of hoped I'd get some word from my only daughter, today of all days.' There were still unopened presents from this morning, any one of them might have been from Molly but of course Gran would not touch them. She would not even let Lambkin open them for her. 'No, it's too late now, girlie, I haven't got the heart. Everything's slipping away. Come the morning and I won't be a burden to any of you any more...' And with that she turned away and would not say another word.

Meanwhile, in Helen's kitchen, Roger was spooning extra sugar into his cocoa although to be fair his thoughts were still with Gran.

'You know,' he said, 'she's a nasty ungrateful old woman and she smells so bad most people think she's dead already, but in a funny sort of way I shall miss her.' Helen was moved.

'Oh Roger, will you really?' Roger licked the spoon.

'No. I just thought I'd try it, see how it sounded.' Lawrence thought they were all giving up too easily.

'Surely there must be something we can do?' Roger looked doubtful.

'Tricky one, old chap. You see, she's absolutely certain she's been cursed, so unless we can convince her otherwise, I rather think it's "goodnight Vienna".' And he smiled happily to himself. Helen was just about to have a little word about caring and sharing when there was a quiet knock on the kitchen door.

'Who on earth can that be at this hour?' She looked at Roger.

'Well, I told Lambkin to come over if she got any worse...'

'Oh Roger,' said Helen, 'you don't think...' But when the door opened, there stood Plato Potatos looking very miserable indeed. 'Oh Plato, come in,' said Helen. 'We thought you were someone else.' Plato looked around.

'No, is no one else, it is I, Plato Potatos. I close my Funspot but I cannot go home.' Absentmindedly, he pulled the chair from under Lawrence and sat down. 'Tell me, how is Missis Pirate? She come to my place for Happy Birthday and all she get is lousy time and a pudding on the bonce. I hate myself.'

'No, no, my dear chap,' said Roger, 'you mustn't blame yourself.' Plato shook his head.

'I cannot help it. It is how I feel. So tell me if there is anything I can do, and I do it.'

'Nice thought, old chap. But it wouldn't work I'm afraid. You see, Missis Pirate is already turning up her toes.' Plato looked blank. 'Shuffling off the mortal coil, popping her sea boots, so to speak.'

'Missis Pirate is dying?'

'Oh yes,' said Roger rubbing his hands, 'good as in the ground. So, "no go, Plato" I'm afraid. Still, mustn't brood. More cocoa, anyone?' That was when Lawrence had one of his extra-brilliant ideas.

'Just a minute, Mr Bones. Gran thinks Mr Potatos gave her the Black Spot, right?' Plato nodded in agreement.

'Oh yes, she call me "Blind Poo" and grab me here...' and he showed Helen the red finger-marks on his neck.

'So if Gran thinks he's the one who put the curse on her...' Lawrence was thinking aloud but Roger was already ahead of him.

'...Then you think he might be the one to lift it?' Roger's face became grim. 'Blast it, Lawrence, it's a devilish long-shot but knowing that woman's luck it might just work.' Lawrence pushed his glasses up his nose and turned to Plato.

'Mr Potatos, we've had an idea. There might be something you can do after all.'

The full moon was casting long shadows down Wordsworth Close as Lawrence Kitten, his baseball jacket fastened right up to his chin and his chin tucked deep inside a warm scarf, waited for Lambkin Bones. He looked at his watch, almost half past twelve, what on earth was keeping her? Then one of the dark shadows in the doorway of the Pirates' house got even darker and turned into Lambkin, trying very hard to close the front door without making a sound.

'Where have you been? Is everything all right?' Lambkin was wearing a jacket with the collar turned up so far, he could hardly see her face.

'Gran wouldn't go to sleep. Said it's a waste of time if she's doomed anyway.' Lawrence had to admit the old woman had a point.

'What did you do?' he asked

'I left her in her hammock singing "Abide with me" and told her I was going to stay over at your house. Dad and Man-in-the-Sack have gone to bed.' Just then, as if jerked by an unseen hand, a mysterious cloaked figure flew across the gateway and disappeared from view in a clatter of dustbins.

'Ow! Stand still, please. Nice doggy,' said a voice Lambkin thought she knew.

Plato Potatos was draped from head to foot in what looked like red velvet curtains and was trying to untangle himself from a large excited dalmatian on a lead.

'I don't believe this,' said Lambkin.

'You're not the one who has to,' Lawrence reminded her.

'Hey, Lawrence,' said Plato. 'We been waiting here twenty minutes. You know is nearly two hours in doggy time?'

'What's he doing with a dog?' asked Lambkin in despair. Plato looked offended.

'I am Blind Poo, yes? I come with Black Spot, yes? Well, this is black spotty guide dog. Hey, Lawrence, you like the cloak? Funspot curtains, good eh?'

'Come on,' said Lambkin grimly, 'let's get it over with.'

They told Plato to knock on the front door and shout for 'Abigail Blood'. They would hide out of sight and tell him what to say. Plato knocked and sort of shouted but he was far too polite and quiet about it.

The door remained firmly shut.

'She'll never hear that,' said Lambkin.

'Louder!' said Lawrence and this time Plato used the voice he reserved for customers who complained about his cooking.

'Abigail Blood!!' The words boomed down one side of Wordsworth Close then echoed all the way back up the other side and rattled the windows of the houses opposite. Plato seemed pleased with the effect. 'Hey, Lawrence, is okay for you?' But at that moment the door swung open behind him and there stood Gran. 'Aah! Missis Pirate!' squeaked Plato and quickly scuttled out of range in case the old devil was armed.

He need not have worried, poor Gran was a changed woman. All the fight had gone out of her. Standing there on the doorstep in her nightie and sea boots with her hair on end, she suddenly looked quite small and pathetic.

'Yes?' she said in a quavery old voice. 'What is it?' Plato stood on tiptoe and tried to look impressive and ghostly.

'Ooo,' he wailed, 'I am Blind Pooo!'

'Oh, you look different,' said Gran peering at him. 'Have you come for me?' Fortunately a handy cloud covered the moon at that moment and Plato was able to seek help.

'Hey, Lawrence!' he whispered in a panic. 'What I say now?'

'Say, "I have travelled many miles over land and sea."' Plato put on his spookiest voice and waved his

arms about like a demented starfish.

'I have travelled many miles over land and sea...'
He paused and wailed a bit more until Lawrence
came up with the next line.

'To bring you this message,' said Lawrence.

'To bring you this message,' said Plato.

'What message?' asked Gran. Plato gave a sickly
grin and shrugged spookily.

'She want to know what message,' he whispered
desperately out of the corner of his mouth.
Lawrence turned to Lambkin.

'What message?'

'How do I know what message?' said Lambkin.

'You're a Pirate,' said Lawrence. 'Think of
something!'

'Hey, kiddies,' said Plato. 'Any time you're ready
is good for me...'

'The Black Spot was never meant for you,' said
Lambkin at last. Plato did some more wailing to
recapture the mood which he felt had fallen off
slightly.

'Ooooo, the Black Spotty was never meant for
you.'

'There was a mix-up with the menus.'

'There was a mix-up with the menus, waaaah,
oooo!'

'It was meant for the fat woman at the other table
with the ugly children!'

'Wooo, aaaah, it was meant for the fat woman at

the next... Hey, are you kidding me?' Plato was willing to try anything once, but this was stretching it a bit. Lambkin was determined.

'...At the other table with the ugly children! Trust me!' Plato shrugged.

'...At the other table with the ugly children! Oooo, wahhh.' The effect was like magic. Gran gasped once and disappeared inside, slamming the door behind her. Plato pulled off his red velvet hood and hurried over to the children. 'Hey, kiddies, she have to be one crazy old lady to fall for that, eh?' Lawrence could not have agreed more, nobody in their right mind would believe that load of old nonsense. Even the dalmatian looked suspicious.

Then they heard the firing of a flintlock pistol and Gran's voice raised in a joyful sing-song.

'Alive, alive-oo, alive, alive-oo! I'm free! Nobody wants to kill me!' and she let rip with her other pistol.

'I'll accept apologies from both of you,' said Lambkin smugly and with the dalmatian barking happily at their heels, they all scurried off to Lawrence's house before the neighbours called the police.

5
An Unexpected Visitor

Gran was dancing round and round. She had wedged a chair under the handle of the living-room door so no one could spoil her fun and now she was leaping and capering, firing her pistols in all directions. Then, during a brief pause to catch her breath and re-load, she noticed a strange noise, a sort of ringing noise which seemed to be coming from the birthday presents on the table.

Sure enough, in the middle of the table beneath a mound of torn wrapping paper, a big unopened bottle was definitely making a ringing noise. Now to Gran's way of thinking bottles had no business ringing. If bottles had a job in life it was to lie quiet and mind their manners until someone wanted a nip o' grog or decided to smash them open for a prezzie. This bottle was being cheeky and she decided to teach it a lesson.

First she threatened it with her cutlass. (People or things, it made no difference to Gran. In her experience cold steel was a universal language.) But the bottle ignored her. If anything, the ringing got slightly louder. Next she showed it both flintlocks, primed and loaded. The bottle changed its tone as if it were actually laughing at her.

That was when she decided to go for the blunderbuss. (The natural choice when firepower

48

really matters.) Gran's blunderbuss was called Betsy and was a bit like a shotgun except that where the barrel should have been there was an enormous bell-shaped brass mouth down which you could stuff whatever you had to hand, rusty nails, broken glass, the odd dead cat... That was the beauty of it. So long as you used enough black powder to give it all a good lift, old Betsy would do the rest.

Gran put in three big measures of powder then loaded up with bent teaspoons, the spare set of false teeth and the broken glass from old Kate's prezzie. Then she put the bell of the blunderbuss against the ringing bottle, closed her eyes and fired.

There was an almighty bang and when she opened her eyes the bottle had disappeared. All that was left was a cloud of smoke, a funny smell and some bits of brown paper – oh, and a ringing noise, only now it was coming from behind an old ship's wheel on the other side of the room.

Drawing her dagger, Gran tracked it down to a small black box which apart from having her false teeth embedded in it, also had several rows of buttons and a sort of flap which Gran lifted gingerly with the tip of her dagger.

The ringing stopped so suddenly it made her jump and then out of the silence she heard this:

'Happy Birthday to you, Happy Birthday to you, Happy Birthday old ratbag...' That did it, as soon as she heard that, Gran knew it could only mean one thing.

'Molly!' she shouted. 'You remembered!' And such an unusual prezzie too, a personalised music box! Then she nearly fell over because the box spoke to her.

'So what are you waiting for, Mother?' said the mobile phone, 'Come to the door and let me in, it's freezing out here.'

Molly Blood was tall and fierce with tumbling auburn hair and sparkling green eyes. She also had a laughing red mouth and a lot of sharp white teeth. After she and Gran had exchanged traditional Pirate arm-locks, Molly used her teeth to pull the cork from a grog bottle which appeared like magic from inside her coat. She spat the cork at Pustule, took a huge swig, then held out the bottle to Gran.

'Not for me thanks, Moll,' said Gran burping meekly. 'Roger doesn't like me drinking rum after midnight.'

'Hah!' said Molly in disgust. 'That man should be slung up by his underpants till his tongue turns black and his eyeballs pop!'

'Mm, so no plans to get back together then?' Gran looked nervously at the ceiling and wished Molly would keep her voice down. Gunfire in the small hours was one thing but entertaining Roger's ex-wife in the dead of night was entirely another.

'Listen, Mother, I want to see the nippers and I

need your help, or have you gone soft in your old age?' Gran looked hurt.

'Nah, you know me, Moll. Say what you want and it's as good as done.' Molly leaned across the table.

'I want you to get rid of Roger. Think you can you do that for me?' At once Gran began to roll up her sleeves.

'No problem at all, I'll go and strangle him now if you want!' And she scampered off so fast Molly only just managed to grab the back of her nightie.

'No, Mother, I don't want you to strangle him!'

'Well, there's always poison, that's slower of course. Or…I could fill his hammock with gunpowder and drop a lighted match down his jim jams…' Molly took her mother gently by the throat and squeezed until she stopped talking.

'Listen, Mother, I know you can barely keep track of your own saliva these days but try and concentrate. I do not want you to kill Roger.' Gran's face fell. 'I just want you to keep him out of the way. Tomorrow morning. Can you do that?' Gran mouthed silently until Molly released the pressure.

'Be *easier* to kill him,' she gasped. 'He's a bit of an old sly boots.' Molly began to tighten her grip. 'But I'll think of something! You just leave it to me.' Molly handed her the mobile phone.

'I'll be in touch,' Molly promised and giving Gran a last affectionate dead leg was gone, leaving

52

her to limp about wondering how on earth she would keep her part of the bargain.

The following morning, when Lambkin Bones got back from Lawrence's house, she heard Gran singing in the kitchen. 'Ah, bless her!' she thought. 'Overcome with the joy of not being doomed.' Then she sniffed. A strange and pungent aroma was drifting from the kitchen. 'Good grief!' thought Lambkin. 'Unless I'm very much mistaken, and I don't think I am, that's one of Gran's special breakfasts. We *are* honoured. She should get the Black Spot more often.'

Gran was stirring a Special Stew in her big black Special Stewpot. Every so often she stopped singing and had a quick taste.

'Mm,' she said thoughtfully as Lambkin came in. 'Not quite right...Needs a little something.' A sudden movement on the workbench caught her eye and quick as a nettled ferret she struck out with an old mesh fly-swat. 'There's a little something!' she shouted gleefully, 'and there's another little something...' She lifted up her victims and examined them. 'Eeny, meeny, miney, mo, catch a weevil by the toe...'

'Weevils don't have toes,' Lambkin pointed out.

Gran looked. 'Stupid girl, it's only a figure of speech.'

(Weevils are a type of beetle and their young, the

larvae, look like maggots and burrow into anything they want to eat. In the old days, they burrowed into ship's biscuits, which shows how hard-nosed they are. Old Pirates would tap their biscuits on the table and when the weevil grubs dropped out, save them for later to eat with a spoon. In fact long after science had cured the weevil menace, Pirates continued to treat the little devils as a delicacy. Much as Scottish people continue to eat haggis long after the need to consume anything so revolting has passed. But we digress...)

'Meeny, miney, moany, moo,' said Gran choosing the smaller of the two wriggling creatures. 'Tough luck, sucker, and into the stew!' At that moment Roger arrived and Gran quickly hid the other weevil behind her back.

'Good morning, good morning,' said Roger cheerily. 'And what has the Queen of the Kitchen got for us today? One of her Specials I'll be bound.' After all the terrible noises in the night, it was encouraging to find his mother-in-law trying to make amends.

'Nothing's too good for my favourite son-in-law,' Gran simpered, patting him affectionately with the stew ladle.

'Watch her, Dad,' said Lambkin. 'She's up to something.' Gran glared at her but Roger was too busy tasting the stew on his sleeve to notice.

'Oh, Mother-in-Law, *c'est magnifique!* You've excelled yourself. How does she do it, eh,

Lambkin?' Gran kept her weevil hand firmly out of sight. 'Come on, now,' said Roger, 'out with it. What have you put in there, eh? What's that you're hiding?' Gran quickly popped the weevil in her mouth and showed Roger her empty hand, which of course fooled nobody. 'Mother-in-Law, that wasn't a weevil, was it?' Gran shook her head.

'Nnn, mmm, gnnn,' she said innocently and scurried off into the living room taking the stewpot with her.

'The lesser of two weevils actually,' whispered Lambkin.

'I thought as much.' Roger chased after her and peered closely into the pot. 'And what are those crunchy things on top that look like toe-nail clippings?'

'Toe-nail clippings,' said Gran, swallowing hard. Roger stepped back.

'Brilliant! You cooks and your secret ingredients. Hats off, eh, Lambkin? Come on, let's get to the table. I'm starving!' Gran smiled indulgently.

'That's right, you sit yourself down. A man needs a proper breakfast, particularly when he's going to be *spending the whole morning out of doors!*' Roger looked at Lambkin.

'*I'm* going to be spending the morning out of doors?'

'Are you?' said Gran, ladling stew. 'That's a very good idea. You need to get out more.' What was the old minke whale going on about?

'And where would you like me to go, Mother-in-Law?' Probably best to humour the old halibut, after all she *had* cooked the breakfast. Gran handed him a bowl.

'You could go for a walk in the country,' she said, 'Poland for instance, that's a nice country... Or Switzerland, you could learn to yodel... Good gracious me, is that the time?' She whisked Roger's bowl from under his nose but before he could put up a fight, he was distracted by a funny ringing noise.

'What's that noise?'

'What noise?' asked Gran, throwing his bowl over her shoulder.

'Sort of ringing noise,' said Lambkin, looking under the table.

It was the mobile phone but for the life of her, Gran could not remember which of her many pockets she had put it in so she began slapping her sides more or less at random in the hope of hitting the 'off' switch. Naturally the others stared at this strange performance, so she was forced to turn it into a sort of Tyrolean dance, desperately slapping herself and singing 'High on a Hill Stood a Lonely Goatherd...'

Just when she was running out of words, thankfully she felt a familiar lump in her back pocket and punched the phone into silence. 'Did I ever tell you,' she asked as she rubbed her bruised bottom, 'that I was the woman who shot the lonely goatherd? But that's another story…' She hauled Roger to his feet and began frogmarching him towards the door. 'Off we go!' she shouted cheerfully. 'No time to lose if you want to be in Switzerland before the pubs shut.' Roger fought himself free.

'Mother-in-Law, I've no idea what all this is about but you're wasting your time. As it happens I have my own plans for this morning.' Gran seized him by the collar, pulled him very close and stared at him hard with her one good eye.

'Plans?' she whispered. 'What sort of plans? Do they…involve being out of doors all morning?'

'Well yes,' Roger admitted, 'yes they do as a matter of fact.'

'Oh, well that's all right then,' said Gran, mightily relieved. 'Off you go! Have a nice time! Don't forget to write!' And she bundled the poor man out of the house and slammed the door.

The moment she was back in the living room, Gran whipped out her mobile phone as if she had been using such things all her life, and would actually have looked quite cool if she had not been holding it upside down so that the flap covered her nose.

'Red Mother to Red Leader,' she said in a hoarse whisper. 'All clear, I repeat, all clear!' Lambkin was determined to get to the bottom of this.

'What *are* you up to? Who's that you're talking to?' Gran pocketed the phone and smiled a secret smile.

'For me to know and you to find out,' she said annoyingly.

'Well it can't be a friend,' said Lambkin, 'you haven't got any...' Gran tapped the side of her nose.

'Least said, soonest mended.' She was full of these sayings and could keep it up for hours.

'Come on, what are you doing with a mobile phone? Hey, you're not a drug dealer, are you?' Gran folded her arms and looked smug.

'Many a mickle makes a muckle.' Lambkin gave up and helped herself to some stew.

6
Black Alan

Later that morning, the peace and quiet of Wordsworth Close was shattered by the arrival of a huge Harley Davidson motorbike. It roared and clattered up to the Pirates' house where, with a last huge roar for luck, the rider let the engine die and had a good look around.

He was tall and mean-looking and very black. His leather clothes were black, his Harley Davidson was black and his name was Black Alan. The only colourful thing about him was the reflection of his passenger in his mirrored sunglasses. She wore buckskin knee breeches and a bright red shirt with an embroidered sash and when she took off her helmet a mass of auburn hair fell rollicking free.

Of course it was Molly Blood. She handed her helmet to Black Alan, threw a big leather duffle bag across her shoulder and strode up to the Pirates' front door.

Inside, Man-in-the-Sack had just got Baby off to sleep when he heard a sound that fair made his tripes turn over. Living ashore he had grown used to doorbells and telephones which had made him jump at first, but it was a long time since he had heard the traditional two kicks, one thump and a cry of 'Stand by to get pillaged!' which could mean only one thing – a nasty attack of the Bloods.

He ran to the front door only to be flattened against the wall as Molly burst it open.

'Well, well, well, Man-in-the-Sack,' she said as he slid gently to the floor. 'No one stuffed a sofa with you yet?' and she stepped over him as Gran appeared from the living room wiping her hands on a blood-stained pinny.

'You've caught me on the hop,' she said as Molly put her in a traditional Pirate half-Nelson. 'I was just fixing the littleun's victuals...' Molly tightened her grip.

'Taken care of my dear ex-husband?' Gran broke free.

'No problems there, Moll, nice as pie!' she said and head-butted her daughter gaily. They sea-horsed around for a bit, punching each other affectionately and tripping over Man-in-the-Sack until they heard Lambkin calling down from her bedroom.

'What's going on, Gran? Who is it?' Gran gave Molly a playful forearm jab and straightened her pinny.

'Why don't you come down and see for yourself, my precious?' The two of them waited like giggling schoolgirls until Lambkin appeared at the top of the stairs. For a long time Lambkin looked at her mother.

'Mum?' She could not believe her eyes.

'Hello, love,' said Molly quietly.

'Mum, Mum, Mum, Mum, MUM!' shouted Lambkin and launched herself down the stairs and into her mother's outstretched arms.

'All Bloods together, eh girls?' whooped Gran. 'Bloods and proud of it!' And to celebrate she drop-kicked poor Man-in-the-Sack, who was just getting to his feet, and as they both crash-landed on the floor, Gran idly wondered how Roger was getting on in Switzerland.

In all his years at sea, Roger Bones had never quite got to grips with reading. Pirates are not great letter-writers, unless you count ransom notes and let's face it, there is very little to read at the end of a cutlass, beyond 'Made in Sheffield' possibly.

But life ashore was a different matter. Reading, Roger felt, would give him the edge in those tricky situations where swordplay never quite did the trick – the checkout at Sainsbury's say, or if he took Helen to the Greek Funspot. A chap should at least be able to order a couple of kebabs. But how to get started?

It was Lawrence who came to the rescue. He still had his first reading books up in the loft and was sure he could get Mr Bones started in next to no time. He even made some special flash-cards based on a restaurant menu.

Far from going to Switzerland, Roger had not even got to the end of Wordsworth Close. While

Helen was at weight-training with her friend Stephanie, Roger and Lawrence were in the kitchen getting stuck into some serious reading.

'"Where...is...Spot?"' Roger traced the words carefully. '"N...N...N..."'

'Naughty,' said Lawrence helpfully.

'"Naughty". Thank you, Lawrence.' Roger kept his finger on the page so as not to lose his place. '"Naughty Spot. It... is... dinner... time. Where can he be? Is he be... be...hind the door?"' Roger lifted the flap on the page. He enjoyed this bit. '"No."' He winked at Lawrence. '"Is he inside the clock?" Silly question, eh Lawrence? No dog in his right mind would go inside a clock.'

The picture in the book showed a grandfather clock with a flap in its front which Roger lifted.

'Good grief!' he shouted, elbowing Lawrence hard in the ribs. 'There's a snake inside the clock! Lawrence! These people keep snakes in their clocks! Look...' Lawrence sighed. To think he had been worried that *Where's Spot?* might not be grown-up enough.

'Mr Bones,' he said, 'you've obviously got the hang of this. I think we should move on.' Roger's face fell.

'Can't we just find out where Spot is?'

'Look, I thought you wanted to be able to read a restaurant menu?'

'You're right, Lawrence, you're right.' Roger

closed the book. 'Hit me with the flash-cards.' Lawrence picked up the bundle and faced him across the table.

'All right, Mr Bones. You're in the restaurant with Mum. The waiter brings the menu and you see this...' He held up a card which said 'Vegetable of the Day' but Roger was not even watching. He was busy trying to sneak a look at the last page of *Where's Spot?*

'Mr Bones?' The book snapped shut and Roger looked guilty but relieved.

'He was in his basket all the time. Thank goodness, eh? Mind you, I think his mother should have looked there in the first place...'

'Mr Bones, please!' Lawrence had had enough.

'Sorry, Lawrence, sorry.' He stared dutifully at the flash-card. 'Right, let's see...' He thought hard and tugged at his beard. 'Ve...Vegg...' He closed one eye and squinted. 'Vegget-abubble...' In the end he shook his head. 'You *are* holding it the right way up I suppose?' he asked hopefully.

Molly had brought presents for both the children – clothes for Lambkin, who had rushed off to try them on, but she was not sure about her choice for Baby.

'Do you think he'll like it?' she asked uncertainly. Gran looked at the shrivelled object hanging from the hood of the pram, the lank strands of hair plastered to its puckered features.

'I don't see why not,' she said, 'a shrunken head always makes an acceptable gift. He had a couple last birthday but you can't have too many, can you?' Molly peered into the pram. She had been looking forward to seeing Baby again but now the time had come she felt strangely nervous. At least the child was quiet.

'Has he always been green?'

'Of course he has,' said Gran, 'he's his grandma's little pea-pod pie.' Gentle snores were rattling the hood and the shrunken head stirred mournfully on its thong.

'Why's he hanging upside down?'

'Because he's asleep!' said Gran pushing her aside. 'You are out of touch, aren't you, girl? Here, would you like to hold him?'

'No, no!' said Molly rather too quickly. 'Don't you go disturbing him on my account!'

'You're probably right,' Gran agreed. 'He ate Bubble and Squeak earlier.' Molly looked shocked. Gran shrugged helplessly. 'I know, I know, gerbils always give him wind but what can you do? They're his favourite...'

At that moment Lambkin came in, dressed from head to toe in an exact replica of her mother's costume, even down to a miniature cutlass and grog bottle.

'Well,' she said shyly, 'what do you think?'

'Oh yes!' Molly strode over to her. 'I was guessing at the size but those fit a treat. What do you think, Mother? Mother, whatever's the matter?' At the sight of her daughter and granddaughter together, Gran had come over all weepy and was dabbing her eyes with the shrunken head.

'Just look at her! Every inch her mother's daughter. It does my old heart good.' She sniffed loudly and Lambkin went over and gave her a hug. 'We don't belong ashore, girls, not us!' Gran wiped her nose on the sleeve of her shirt. 'We've no business stuck in a dry berth, with our canvas flapping and our planking warped.' Molly began to look a bit embarrassed but Gran seemed not to notice. 'You know, the sea may be a cruel mistress, but we should never have left her. Why did we do it, eh, Lambkin?'

Now perhaps Gran was not really expecting an answer but Lambkin happened to remember very clearly why they had left the sea.

'Because Mum kicked us off the boat,' she said simply. Molly looked really sheepish, Gran just looked shocked.

'Lambkin Bones that's a terrible thing to say, you apologise to your mother at once...'

'But she did.' Lambkin turned to Molly. 'Don't you remember? You said Baby and me were too young to be Pirates and Gran was too old...' Gran flew at her so fast, Molly only just had time to get

66

between them.

'Ooh, you ungrateful little baggage! Stood standing there in those lovely new togs telling barefaced Big Ones.' And she took a swing at Lambkin with the shrunken head. 'I blame that father of hers, filling her head with land-crabbery.'

'It's all right, Mother,' said Molly but Gran was shouting so loudly Baby had begun to grizzle and things were getting out of hand. 'Look,' said Molly, gently taking Gran aside, 'why don't you take Baby upstairs for a nice game of shove ha'penny, eh? Leave me to have a quiet word with Lambkin.'

'A quiet word? She wants a good talking to!' Molly steered her firmly towards the pram.

'Go on, please. Leave it to me.'

'Kids these days don't know they're born,' Gran grumbled as she swung the pram around. 'In my day if you told Big Ones they skinned you alive, pulled all your teeth out and cast you adrift in an open bucket.' She had absentmindedly begun chewing the shrunken head as if it were an apple. 'It's no wonder we've got Breakfast Television,' she said mysteriously and tossed the rest of the head to Baby.

When they had gone, Molly took Lambkin gently by the hand and sat her down at the table.

'It's high time you and me had a talk,' she said.

'You did say it though, didn't you? About me and Baby and Gran...' Molly looked hard at her daughter and sighed.

'Lambkin,' she said at last. 'I may not have much time for your father but he's right about one thing. The Spanish Main is no place to bring up kids.' Lambkin was going to interrupt but her mother waved her down. 'Don't get me wrong, piracy is a great way of life with much to offer the modern woman. But frankly the hours are terrible and you can't get a decent child-minder for love nor money...'

'What about Gran?' She seemed the obvious choice.

'No, you certainly couldn't get a minder for her,' said Molly, missing the point.

'And that's why you kicked us off the boat.'

'I did not kick you off the boat.' Lambkin could tell her mother was lying. Her cheeks had gone a bit red and she was choosing her words very carefully. 'I simply agreed with your father that until you were a little bit older...'

'Mum,' said Lambkin, 'if you'd ever agreed with Dad it would have been in all the papers. You two couldn't agree on the time of day!' Molly tried to look hurt.

'We've had our differences, I'd be the first to admit it. But we both want what's best for you. One day you're going to make up your own mind but I've been thinking, how are you ever going to know what you want in life if you don't get a taste for seafaring?

Suppose you came back and lived with me, just for a bit? To get the feel of it, so to speak. How does that sound? I bet we'd have a really great time.' Lambkin found it very difficult to know when her mother was serious or when she was just playing games.

'Are you asking me?' Molly's eyes were exactly the same shade of green as Lambkin's and at the moment they looked very cool and level.

'Yes,' she said, 'I'm asking you.'

'I'll have to think about it,' said Lambkin, 'we'll have to talk it over with Dad.' Molly's eyes narrowed and you could tell this was not the answer she wanted, but she hid it very well and nodded in agreement.

7
Lambkin's Choice

Roger Bones had finished his lesson and was on his way home. He was not sure he was ready to tell the Pirates about his reading but Lawrence had told him how important it was to practise and so he had brought the flash-cards with him and was leafing through them as he went along.

'Thank you,' he said, 'I will pay by credit card.' And then he said, 'Yes, I would like to see the sweet trolley...' And then he realised that a large chap on a motorbike was staring at him. Roger shuffled the flash-cards and stared back. Black Alan had been outside the Pirates' house for over an hour now and to tell the truth, he was beginning to feel the cold.

''Scuse me, mate,' he said as Roger passed, 'you haven't got the time, have you?' Roger looked blank. 'Time, you know, tick-tock?' Roger squinted up at the sun.

'Quarter past twelve, about...' Odd, he thought, chap on a motorbike in Wordsworth Close, shivering, asking for the time... He turned up another flash-card. 'Bring me a bread roll,' he said accidentally out loud. The chap on the motorbike took off his sunglasses.

'I've got half a cheese sandwich you can have,' he said. Roger went indoors still trying to decide if the fellow was joking.

Inside, a stranger scene than usual greeted him. Man-in-the-Sack was slumped in one corner of the hallway and Baby, who was making the most horrible slurping noises, had something unpleasant in his pram, something that looked like a very old apple core only bigger. But the strangest thing was Gran. She was bent double and had a large brass megaphone pressed up against the living-room door.

'Mother-in-Law,' said Roger, wrenching the 'apple core' away from Baby and sniffing it suspiciously, 'you don't know anything about a chap on a motorbike, do you?' Gran jumped, took one look at Roger, took another at the living room and went rigid all over.

'Aargh!' she shouted, eyes rolling wildly. 'It's you! You're supposed to be in Switzerland!' Then she clutched at her heart and tried to fall over, but Roger was too quick for her.

'Oh no you don't.' He grabbed her by the collar and took a bite from the apple, mm, chewy but not unpleasant... 'Who's that chap outside?'

Gran put the megaphone to her ear.

'Pardon?'

'I said, "Who's that chap...?" Come off it. What were you listening to just now?'

'Pardon?' Roger pushed her to one side and made for the living room, but with a nimbleness surprising in one so wrinkly, Gran hurled herself across his path and yelled through the megaphone.

'Red Mother to Red Leader!'

'What's going on?' Roger's eyes narrowed dangerously. 'Who have you got in there?' But Gran just flapped her arms and began to shout even louder, her voice rising in a panicky high-pitched sing-song.

'Red Leader! Red Leeeader! Bandits at twelve o'clock!'

'It's quarter past actually.' Roger was rapidly losing patience. 'I've been out all morning and I want to know what's going on in there!' Gran stood firm, like George Washington beside his apple tree or perhaps the boy on the burning deck 'when all save he had fled'.

'Shan't tell!' she declared stoutly.

'Mother-in-Law...'

'Never! My lips are sealed! Wild horses would not drag it out of me.'

'I'll double your rum ration,' said Roger quietly. The effect was uncanny.

'It's our Molly,' said Gran. 'She's trying to get Lambkin to leave home.'

'Right!' said Roger, lifting her up and bumping open the living-room door with her.

Lambkin and Molly were both staring at Roger when he entered with Gran tucked under one arm like a roll of carpet. Lambkin looked guilty but Molly did not look guilty at all. It was a long time since Roger had seen them both together and he had forgotten how alike they were.

'Well, well, well,' said Molly, getting slowly to her feet. 'Isn't it amazing the people you meet when you haven't got a gun?'

'I couldn't help it, Moll,' Gran snivelled, 'he beat it out of me.'

'Typical!' said Molly.

'Rubbish!' said Roger, dropping Gran on the floor and marching over to Molly. 'Now listen you, I demand to know what you've been…?' Lambkin pushed herself between them. Why was it always like this the moment her parents clapped eyes on each other?

'Excuse me you two, have you met? Dad this is Mum, Mum this is Dad. I'm your daughter, Lambkin. Remember?' Roger came to his senses and made a big effort to be civilised.

'I'm sorry, Lambkin, you're right of course. No excuse for bad manners. Hello, Molly.' Molly showed a few of her sharp white teeth, though you could hardly have called it a smile.

'Hello, Roger.'

'How's life on the ocean wave?'

'Oh, up and down, you know.'

'Mm, killed anyone recently?'

'That's it!' Molly snarled, showing a few more teeth. 'Enough of the polite conversation!' Lambkin could see it was pretty hopeless but nevertheless she

tried to smooth things over.

'Dad...Mum's got this idea she'd like...well, we'd *both* quite like you to think it over.' She glanced across at Molly but her mother was giving nothing away, so Lambkin ploughed on. 'We were wondering how you'd feel if...or to put it another way...' Molly was not used to all this pettifogging pussy-footing. Why couldn't the girl get to the point?

'Look, Roger,' Molly interrupted, 'I'm out of here tomorrow and Lambkin's coming with me. You got anything to say about that?'

'Great, Mum,' said Lambkin. 'That's great!' Even by Molly's standards it was pretty crude. Roger stared at them as if someone had just drenched him in cold seawater.

'You're joking.'

'I never joke,' said Molly.

'Sorry,' said Roger, 'I forgot.' But it was all coming back to him pretty quickly. 'Look, if you want to take someone to sea, take your mother, take Pustule, but you're not taking Lambkin, it's not fair!'

'Fair!' Molly snorted, looking around her. 'You call this fair? This is no life for a Pirate, living here in this...this...'

'House?' Roger suggested.

'House!' spat Molly, as if it were a ship-load of seasick camels on a very hot day. 'Eating regular meals, going to school, making friends. It's disgusting! She should be back with her own people where she belongs.'

'Her own people!' It was Roger's turn to snort. 'Like that weirdo on the motorbike I suppose?'

'You leave Black Alan out of this!' roared Molly.

'Black Alan? Black Alan?!' They were nose to nose across the table. Lambkin forced her way between them.

'Stop it! Stop it, both of you! Can't you ever discuss things without fighting?' Molly and Roger thought about this, but Lambkin was spot on, they couldn't.

Half an hour later, they were *still* fighting. Arm wrestling and still snarling at each other through clenched teeth, while Gran dozed in her hammock.

'So who's this Black Alan when he's afloat?' grunted Roger.

'A friend, just a friend...' Beads of sweat glistened on their faces and their clasped hands quivered with the effort.

'Oh yes,' Roger gritted, 'and how long before my daughter's expected to call this "friend" Daddy?'

'*Your* daughter!' Molly almost lost her grip. 'She's my daughter too, you know. Anyway, I've been hearing all about you and the land-crab from next door.' That did it. Roger's eyes flashed.

'You leave Helen out of this!' he shouted and just

for a split second his concentration slipped. His arm went crashing to the table, twisting his elbow quite painfully. Molly roared with laughter and Gran woke up to see what the fuss was about. 'Best out of five?' winced Roger.

'Go on, killer,' said Molly flexing her muscles till the tattoos danced and all the little ginger hairs stood up on her arm. 'Give me your best shot'. Even Gran found this hard to believe, they had been at it for ages.

'Stop it, the pair of you!' she shouted. 'This is just what Lambkin was talking about. Can't you see you're driving the child away?' And she pointed at the door where sure enough, a notice saying 'Driven Away – Lambkin' had been spiked with a dagger. 'You should be settling your differences like sensible grown-ups, not brawling like a couple of old trollops in a dockside bar!' All of a sudden Lambkin's parents felt terribly ashamed of themselves.

'You're right, you know, Mother,' said Molly.

'Yes, Mother-in-Law, you're right,' said Roger. 'What do you suggest? We put ourselves entirely in your hands.' There was just a trace of a smile between Gran and Molly which unfortunately Roger was too busy massaging his elbow to notice.

'Right!' said Gran. 'Then follow me…'

In fact, Lambkin had only gone next door for some peace and quiet, and was playing cards with

Lawrence and Black Alan. On the way over she had found Black Alan shivering on his motorbike and had discovered that in spite of the way he looked, he was not mean at all, just cold and a bit moody. Now he was sitting at the kitchen table, wrapped in Lawrence's Jurassic Park duvet, while Lambkin dealt the cards.

Normally she liked nothing better than a good game of pontoon, particularly when she was banker, but today her heart was not in it. She was still thinking about Roger and Molly. If Molly was serious, she really might have to decide whether to go with her mum or stay with her dad, although right at that moment she did not particularly feel like seeing either of them ever again.

'What will you do?' asked Lawrence, trying to sound unconcerned but secretly hoping she would stay. Lambkin frowned.

'I don't know,' she said at last. 'What do you think, Black Alan? Shall I stay here or shall I come and live with you and Mum?' In the warm kitchen, Black Alan's sunglasses had steamed up and he was trying to polish them on the tablecloth without letting the children see his cards.

'Don't ask me,' he said, 'I don't live with your mum. She just stays round my place when she comes ashore.'

'So you're not a Pirate then?' Lawrence was surprised.

'No way!' said Black Alan. 'I can't stand water, me. I'm from Solihull.' When Lambkin heard this she threw her cards down on the table.

'There, you see!' Roger had assumed Molly and Black Alan were living together. 'That's my dad, jumping to conclusions, getting everything wrong. He wouldn't even listen to what Mum had to say.' Lawrence tried to see both sides, remembering how things were when his parents were splitting up. They had fought all the time and had often said things they did not mean, what grown-ups would call 'being childish' really. But if Lambkin was planning to leave home, Lawrence guessed Roger might be feeling a bit hurt as well. He tried to point this out but Lambkin was not really listening.

'It's *my* life!' she said. 'Why don't they ever ask *me* what *I* want? It's not my fault they've split up! Now I can't even visit my own mother without World War Three breaking out!' Black Alan looked at her over the top of his cards.

'You should think yourself lucky,' he said. 'I used to *wish* my parents would split up.'

'Why?' asked Lawrence. 'Did they fight a lot?'

'All the time,' said Black Alan. 'With me, like, not with each other. And they could be very underhand, sort of sly, you know? I'll give you an example. When I was fifteen, right, I went to Hartlepool to see Chain Saw Jugglers, the Leaking Binbag Tour as I recall... Anyway, you know what they did while I was away?' The children shook their heads. 'They emigrated.' The children stared. 'Underhand, see?'

'What did you do?' Lambkin could think of nothing else to say.

'I moved my bike into the front room,' said Black Alan proudly. 'Better than carrying it up and down stairs all the time,' he explained. Lawrence felt they were straying from the subject.

'Look,' he turned to Lambkin, 'if you're going to go with your mum, you've got to tell your dad. You've *got* to make him listen to you.'

'Get real,' said Lambkin, 'you know what it's like trying to talk to parents when they're arm wrestling.' Lawrence actually had no idea but Black Alan nodded sympathetically.

'Look,' he said, 'from what I saw of your dad, they've very likely finished by now. I mean, no offence, but your mum'll have decked him in the first five minutes.' Lambkin did not say anything but thought that was probably true. 'Your mate's right,' said Black Alan gently, 'you have to go back. See, end of the day it's your choice, kid. You've got to tell them exactly how you feel.'

8
The Devil's Maypole

When Lambkin, Lawrence and Black Alan arrived outside the Pirates' house they found Gran gazing intently up at the rooftops. At first no one could work out what she was doing and then they saw the ladder leaning up against the wall. At the top of the ladder, a long pole had been slung between Lawrence's house and the Pirates' house. There, five or six metres above the crazy paving, at the height of the gutters, Roger and Molly were sitting astride the pole facing each other. In their left hands they held broad cutlasses with thick brass hand-guards and in their right, small lumpy-looking sacks.

'What's happening?' asked Lawrence. 'What are they doing?' Gran giggled and wafted at Pustule who was trying to climb onto her hat.

'They've decided to settle their differences like responsible adults.'

'Not the Devil's Maypole!' said Black Alan.

'Mm,' thought Gran sidling up to him. 'A fine figure of a man,' even if he did seem a touch goose-pimply for her taste.

'Near as makes no difference,' she said proudly. ''Course, I had to leave out the rancid bear grease and the armadillo down the trousers. Well, that's Tesco's for you, but one does one's best...' She

81

trailed off modestly.

'Patagonian rules?'

'You said it, big boy.' Gran slipped her arm through his. 'Here, are you sure you're warm enough?'

'Oh yes, fine!' said Black Alan quickly. 'Cheers.'

Fortunately at that moment Roger's voice rang out from above.

'Do you think we could get on, please?'

Even from a distance you could tell the Devil's Maypole would be pretty uncomfortable for any length of time, you could also tell from the way Molly casually gripped her cutlass between her teeth and tied back her hair one-handed, that this would not be a problem for Roger who was not going to be up there very long. Gran raised her megaphone.

'The Devil's Maypole will be conducted in strict accordance with Patagonian rules. Three two-minute rounds. No biting or gouging in the first round and cutlasses to be used *underarm* only. Is that clear?'

'Oh get on with it!' shouted Roger but Gran was enjoying herself.

'No more than *five* bricks, that's *five* bricks, per sack and may the best woman, sorry *person,* may the best person win.' She trotted over to the house and gave three loud rings on the ship's bell fixed to the wall.

Immediately Molly launched a blistering attack, biffing and bashing for all she was worth and all poor Roger could do was hold up his cutlass and try to get as much of himself as possible behind the hand-guard. Molly swung all the harder until even Gran began to wince as the crunching brick-filled sack struck home.

'Gran!' shouted Lambkin furiously. 'This isn't fair! You know Dad's got vertigo, he's afraid of heights!'

'Oh, is he?' said Gran, all innocence. 'He never said…' But sure enough, if you looked very carefully you could see that Roger had his eyes tight shut. This meant that on the odd occasion he got a swing in, his chances of connecting were fairly slim, while each time Molly scored a direct biff, which was roughly every three seconds, he seemed certain to topple off the pole. In fact, Molly was having to biff from alternate sides, just to straighten him up and make a fight of it, which Gran thought was very sporting of her.

Lambkin realised what her father must be going through. In a way she supposed she should feel grateful that he was suffering so much on her account, but at the same time she hated to see either of them fighting and knew that if it had not been over her, it would have been over something else.

'Dad!' She shaded her eyes.

'Lambkin, is that you?' Roger was not certain. He

still had his eyes shut and his ears were ringing from all the biffing.

'Dad, you don't have to do this you know!' Molly's sack landed smack on the top of Roger's head. She had changed angles because her arm had started to ache.

'Pax, Molly!' Roger yelled. She ignored him and biffed again. 'I said "Pax"!' Roger started swinging so wildly, Molly had to lock cutlasses to stop him falling. 'Lambkin's talking to me. What's the matter with you, woman?'

'Listen, both of you!' said Lambkin. 'Unless you come down, right now, I'm going off with Black Alan and you'll never see me again. Do you understand?'

Molly looked down at her daughter, then across at Roger. With a quick twist of her wrist she sent Roger's cutlass spinning to the ground. He lurched crazily and you could see that one more good biff would see him off. Molly began to heft her sack which was already starting to split at the seams from the punishment it had taken. Lambkin's voice stopped her in mid-swing.

'I mean it!'

'Are you sure about this?' Molly sounded disappointed. 'I can have him off in a second,' and to prove it she rapped Roger's knuckles with the flat of her cutlass, causing him to drop his sack and wobble violently.

'Mum!' Lambkin yelled as she dodged the falling sack. Molly shrugged.

'Stand back,' she shouted and let her own sack and cutlass fall crashing to the ground. Gran was disappointed.

'Kids these days, eh? No sense of fun!' She giggled coyly as she pinched Black Alan's cheek.

Molly swung her leg over the pole and was making her way towards the ladder when she realised that Roger was not following. During the biffing he had relied quite heavily on the cutlass and sack to help keep his balance. With his arms suddenly free, he found the best plan was to lean forward and wrap them, huggy-bear fashion, around the pole. Then he discovered it was quite comforting to put his thumb in his mouth and the longer he lay there, the more comforting it seemed and the less he felt like moving.

'Come on, Roger,' said Molly, 'time to go below.' But the very thought of moving made Roger want to whimper, and so he did. Molly thought he was playing for sympathy. 'Roger! Stop messing about.'

'Ang ot!' said Roger. Then he took his thumb out of his mouth. 'I'm not!' he said. 'It's my vertigo. I don't think I can move... As a matter of fact, I rather think I'm having a panic attack...' And he began to scream very loudly, '*AARGH! AARGH! AARGH!*' and then '*NRNG! NRNG! NRNG!*' as he put his thumb back in his mouth.

'Roger! Stop it!' Molly knew all about hysteria. Like the time she had amputated Toadvine Steevely's left leg with nothing more than a candle stub and a blunt gravy-boat. The important thing with hysteria was to nip it in the bud and keep your gravy-boat out of sight till the last possible moment. 'Take a hold of yourself!' she commanded. Immediately Roger went quiet and stopped hugging the pole. He hugged himself instead but he continued to scream.

'Roger! Listen to me.' Molly edged back towards him. 'I want you to reach out and take my hand. Come on, just reach out...' Roger reached out as best he could but he was still hugging himself and had his eyes closed, so it was not easy. 'You're going to have to open your eyes, Roger,' said Molly patiently. 'I'm over here...' Cautiously Roger opened one eye.

At all costs Molly knew she must hold his gaze. Whatever happened he must not look down.

'Look at me! That's right, keep your eyes on me. Okay, now reach for my hand...' This seemed to do the trick. With his eyes firmly fixed on Molly, Roger slowly inched out until their fingers touched and he was able to clasp her hand. 'Okay,' she said quietly, 'that was the difficult bit, now we're going over to the wall, yes?' Roger nodded meekly but even as he did so his eyes began to wander. 'Keep looking at me!' said Molly sharply. Roger gulped and nodded again. Molly smiled. 'He's all right,' she shouted to the watchers below, 'we're coming down.'

Of course everyone was very relieved and not just the Pirates. Mr Jones from across the road had been jogging by on his way to hockey practice and had stayed to watch. So had Miss Treedle with her little dog, Timmy. In fact quite a crowd had gathered and it was only natural they should clap and cheer when Molly made her announcement. Without thinking Roger let go of her hand to acknowledge the applause. Unfortunately he also looked down.

The smile froze on his face. The faces of the crowd seemed to swim and swirl and his stomach felt like a washing machine on fast spin. He tried to scream but nothing came out and before Molly could grab him he had fallen sideways and was hanging under the pole by his legs. The crowd gasped, all except Miss Treedle who having arrived late, thought Mr Bones was being terribly clever. Then slowly Roger's legs came unstuck and he fell head first into the pile of cutlasses and house bricks littering the crazy paving.

A silence descended on Wordsworth Close broken only by Roger's groans and the sound of Miss Treedle, clapping and shouting, 'Bravo!'

9
Vegetable of the Day

Early the following morning, dressed in the Pirate costume her mother had given her, Lambkin Bones found herself walking down a long echoing hospital corridor searching for Roger's room. She was carrying a big bunch of flowers and a supermarket shopping bag and she was thinking about what the nurse had told her. Roger was not seriously hurt but he had concussion and would be a bit dopey for a while. (Molly had said how would they tell but Lambkin glared at her and tried to pretend she was joking.)

Roger's room was at the very end of the corridor. She peered through the small glass window set high in the door and there he was, lying perfectly still on a starched white bed in a small bare room. His head was covered in a turban of bandages and with his beard, his gold earring and his green hospital nightshirt, the effect was strangely exotic. His breathing was very calm and peaceful and he seemed to be sound asleep.

Lambkin slipped quietly into the room and looked for somewhere to put her flowers. There was a bedside locker with a water jug and an empty glass and at the foot of the bed there was a bare table and that was all. Lambkin poured a glass of water and stuck the flowers in the half empty jug. Then she went to the table and began to unpack her bag.

The nurse had said you should speak to people with concussion even if they did not seem to hear you. Lambkin said she was used to that since her parents never seemed to hear her anyway, but now the time had come, she found it quite hard to strike up a conversation with someone so obviously asleep. She took a deep breath and did her best.

'The nurse says you might not be able to hear me, but I should talk to you anyway. Gran couldn't come...' At the mention of the name 'Gran', Roger's eyelids flickered open although Lambkin was too busy to notice. 'Said she had to stay in and re-arrange her sock drawer.' A snarl curled Roger's lip even though he was only half awake.

Lambkin chattered on, saying whatever came into her head. 'You know they wouldn't let Baby in? They wouldn't even let him on the bus as a matter of fact.' She was holding up an old brown apple core that Roger felt sure he had seen somewhere before. 'He sent you his shrunken head but it looks like someone's been eating it.' Roger remembered where he had seen it before and he closed his eyes and gulped. 'Anyway, I'll put it here,' she placed it gingerly on the table, 'so you can see it when you wake up...Oh, and Lawrence said to bring your flash-cards, just in case you wanted to practise your reading.' Roger closed his eyes quickly. Good grief, he certainly did not feel well enough to explain

about his reading! 'And you're not to be cross with him,' Lambkin went on. 'Maybe I'm not supposed to know about it, but I think it's really good you're learning to read, even if you *are* only doing it so you can take Lawrence's mum to a restaurant.' Roger felt himself go red and kept his eyes tight shut.

'So, that's it then.' Lambkin went over to the bed and laid the flash-cards gently between Roger's folded hands. 'I'll have to be going,' she said. 'Hey, you look better already, your face is all pink.' Then she gave him a quick kiss on the cheek and went to the door. 'Sorry to dash off but Mum's waiting outside. 'Bye, Dad.' And before Roger could say a word, or even open his eyes, she was gone.

Roger sat bolt upright in bed, which was a mistake because it made him feel as if his head were full of red hot weevils trying to force their way out through his eyeballs.

'Lambkin!' he mouthed, clutching his turban, panic stricken at the thought of Molly whisking his only daughter off to the Spanish Main. With his head on fire and with flash-cards flying in all directions, he scrambled out of bed and staggered to the door.

Molly Blood was pacing up and down in the car park when Lambkin came out of the hospital.

'Well?' she said. 'How is he?'

'Still asleep but he's going to be all right.'

Lambkin shouldered her mother's duffle bag and together they set off towards the gate. She saw Molly glance at her watch. 'How are we for time?'

'Fine, don't worry. The Penzance train doesn't leave till eleven.'

At that moment the roar of a Harley Davidson made them both turn round so they did not see Roger, waving frantically at a window behind them. He was pounding on the glass like a madman but the noise was totally drowned by the sound of the approaching motorbike.

Black Alan switched off, smiled at Lambkin and handed Molly her helmet.

'You sure you won't change your mind?' Molly asked, knowing full well what the answer would be.

'I can't, Mum, not now.' Lambkin was almost in tears. 'One day soon maybe, but not now.' Molly took her gently by the shoulders.

'I love you, kid. You know that, don't you?' Lambkin nodded.

'I love you too, Mum.' They hugged each other and for a moment the silence was broken only by a distant banging and the sobs of Black Alan. He was a very emotional person and 'goodbyes' always made him tearful, although when Lambkin looked at him he quickly pretended to be cleaning his wing mirror. 'Goodbye, Black Alan,' she said but he was too choked to reply.

'Come on, let's be off,' said Molly, 'or we'll all be

blubbing.' Lambkin gave her one last hug. 'Go on, girl.' Molly gently pulled away. 'You get back inside. Your father needs you.' Lambkin nodded and with a little smile ran off towards the hospital while Molly swung herself aboard the motorbike.

Roger meanwhile had stopped banging on the window and was trying to work out how three people were going to make their get-away on one motorbike. That was when he realised that Molly was not going to take Lambkin away after all. Before the motorbike could start up again he banged on the window as hard as he could so that even with her helmet on, Molly finally heard him.

She looked round and stared at this demented figure in a green nightshirt and an unravelling turban, holding up a card which said 'Vegetable of the Day'. Roger could tell by the look on her face that something was wrong and fortunately Lambkin arrived at his side to point out the mistake. He threw the card away and held up the only other one he had left. This one said, 'Thank You, I Will Pay by Credit Card'. Molly still looked puzzled until Roger tore off most of it and held up the piece that simply said, 'Thank You'. Molly gave her ex-husband a long level stare with those clear green eyes that were so like Lambkin's, then without warning she stuck out her tongue at them and as the motorbike roared away you could tell she was laughing.

Roger put his arm round Lambkin and they both

watched at the window until long after Molly, Black Alan and the Harley Davidson had disappeared from view.

10
The Season of Goodwill

The months sailed by and soon it was nearly Christmas, the Pirates' first Christmas ashore. Roger was really looking forward to the season of gifts and mellow cheerfulness, which had always been his totally favourite time of the year, and to celebrate he put up an enormous five-metre Christmas tree in the front garden, the biggest Wordsworth Close had ever seen.

Lambkin was happy too. She liked Christmas and although she would not be seeing Molly (who had sent a card from Tristan da Cunha where her ship had put in for repairs) she kept herself busy helping Man-in-the-Sack put up the decorations. Tinsel and streamers, stars and coloured lights, the whole house was transformed. Baby's pram became a Christmas sleigh and the remains of his shrunken head, which he insisted on keeping, were cheered up with a festive tinsel halo.

Even Gran was persuaded to bake a batch of mince pies, though truth to tell she hated Christmas and did not even believe in Santa Claus. This worried Lambkin who had been given the part of Mary in the school nativity and very much wanted the Pirates to see her in her first school play. But with Gran's attitude, it was too much of a risk even to be worth mentioning. It made Lambkin go cold to think of Gran arriving at the school and so she decided to say nothing, then immediately felt guilty in case she had done the wrong thing.

Late one afternoon, a few days before Christmas, Lambkin came home to find Gran bricking up the fireplace, so she stood and watched for a while.

'Gran,' she said at last, 'would you mind telling me what you're doing?' Gran clamped her pipe firmly between her teeth.

'I never liked Christmas,' she said, loading cement on to her trowel, 'not even at sea. But at least there you could drown visitors. That was the beauty of it.'

'It's supposed to be the season of goodwill.'

'Season of goodwill?' Gran snorted. 'Season of begging and scrounging more like. Listen, girlie, if I wanted a smelly old man in a white beard wandering about the place, drinking me grog and going, "Ho ho ho" at three in the morning, I'd ask Vilespleen the Heartless over.'

'But I thought you didn't believe in Father Christmas.' Gran tapped the last brick home.

'I don't,' she said, wiping the trowel on her pinny, 'and just let him try to get his non-existent fat backside down *that* chimney.'

Suddenly Lambkin was sure she had made the right decision about the school play, though admittedly it was tough on Roger. He was feeding a mince pie to Pustule and smiling happily.

'Don't pay any attention to your gran,' he said. Roger had arranged for the vicar to come round later for carol singing with some of the choir and felt sure this would do wonders for her bad attitude. Gran meanwhile had found a bucket of whitewash and was painting slogans on the bricked-up fireplace. 'Push Off Santa', 'Christmas-Free Zone' and 'This Means You, Red Nose' were some of the nicer ones.

'Her bark's far worse than her bite.' Roger's smile became uneasy. 'She'll be right as ninepence once she's had "Ding Dong Merrily" round the old tree.' Lambkin could picture Gran's merry ding-dong only too well, and as for the old tree, it was the wrong one and Roger was barking up it.

She excused herself, saying she had to call for Lawrence, which was true. But what she did *not* say was that they were going back to school, for a rehearsal of the nativity play.

This year it was Miss McGooghan's turn to put on the Christmas play. She was Australian and so she had a lot of unusual ideas. She wanted the nativity to deal with modern issues like homelessness and the destruction of the rainforests. She was also very forceful and all her class had been given parts whether they wanted them or not. All that is except Gail Fleshly. (Creeping Fleshly, the school bully, along with her brothers, Keith and Jason, had once tried to steal the Pirates' treasure.)

Gail would not have been seen dead in a school play even if Miss McGooghan had been crazy enough to suggest it, but for some reason she had taken to spending a lot of time around the rehearsal room, being suspiciously friendly and helpful.

She was there that afternoon when Lambkin and Lawrence arrived, wearing her leather biker's jacket and good-naturedly strangling a shepherd with her Arsenal scarf.

Miss McGooghan was too busy to notice. She was dashing around with a clipboard trying to get everyone into the right theatrical mood.

'Okay, the audience is in. The lights are going down. Kirsty Trivet? Where's Kirsty?' Kirsty was a small girl with very long hair. (If you sat behind her, Lambkin often thought, she looked a lot like Baby's shrunken head.) Kirsty had promised to supply the 'baby' for the nativity. 'Have you brought your Tia Maria?' asked Miss McGooghan. Kirsty held up a doll with blonde curls.

'Actually, Miss, her name's *Tina Marie*.'

'Whatever,' said Miss McGooghan who had a lot on her mind, 'just swaddle her up and stand her by. Here we go then and... cue the music...'

The recorder group started their version of 'Oh Little Town of Bethlehem' (which was quite like their version of 'Camptown Races') and Lambkin got ready for a fast entrance with Lawrence who was playing Joseph.

'And...action!' yelled Miss McGooghan. 'Cue Mary and Joseph!' Lawrence and Lambkin walked on stage arm in arm to the sniggers of Gail Fleshly and her cronies. 'No, no, no, no, no!' Miss McGooghan threw down her clipboard. 'Stop! Listen, Mary and Joseph. I said *Aussie* Rules, OK? So let's get real. Gimme some grit here, some texture. Joseph, you've had a terrible day. You've been travelling since six o'clock this morning, you're tired, you're cold and the donkey's just stood on your foot...Now, where's the Innkeeper?'

'Chicken pox, Miss,' sang out a voice from the back.

'I don't believe it,' said Miss McGooghan, 'they're dropping like flies!' She looked around the room, there was not a lot of choice and time was very short. 'Gail Fleshly? You be the Innkeeper...' Gail smiled a gap-toothed smile and shook her head.

'Sorry, Miss. Can't help you. I'm going to be too busy collecting the ticket money.' Miss McGooghan sat down. Well, it had been a long day and she needed a good laugh.

'So that explains why you've been hanging around. Nice one, Gail,' said Miss McGooghan, 'we all enjoyed that. Putting you in charge of the ticket money would be like putting King Herod in charge of the crèche.'

'Very nice of you to say so, Miss,' said Gail missing the point. Miss McGooghan sprang to her feet.

'Just you get up on that stage and start meeting and greeting!'

Gail began to protest but the door flew open and in walked Mr Spofforth, the Headmaster. He was a tall, thin man with thin grey hair, a thin grey suit and half-rimmed glasses on the end of a thin grey nose. A crumpled and rather grubby Father Christmas costume was dangling from his hand.

'Excuse me, Miss McGooghan,' he said. 'I've been going through the props cupboard. Just look at this, what are we going to do about it?'

'Sorry, Head,' said Miss McGooghan, 'you've lost me.'

'It's filthy.' He held up the offending costume. 'I need it for the Christmas Concert. I always do Father Christmas, don't I, children?'

'Yes, Mr Spofforth,' said the children. Ever since they had been going to St. Bonaventure's they had been answering Mr Spofforth's questions in the same sing-songy chorus and by now they were all very good at it.

'Yes, Mr Spofforth,' repeated Mr Spofforth. 'You see, my Father Christmas is a school tradition.'

'Like lumpy custard,' thought Lawrence glumly.

'Like the nativity play,' said Mr Spofforth

proudly and he beamed at Miss McGooghan.

'Well actually, Head,' Miss McGooghan looked uncomfortable, 'I was sort of hoping we could break with tradition this year, tackle some *issues*...' Mr Spofforth looked at her as if she had appeared suddenly out of thin air.

'Break with tradition? At Christmas? Be serious, Miss McGooghan. Now, come along, what about my costume?'

'Really, Head, I was hoping to avoid that sort of thing.'

'Avoid Father Christmas?' Mr Spofforth peered at her suspiciously. 'You're not a feminist are you, Miss McGooghan? Call us old-fashioned, but over here we rather like Father Christmas, don't we, children?' There was a stony silence. *'Don't we, children?'*

'Yes, Mr Spofforth,' came the ragged reply.

'That's right,' said Mr Spofforth. 'I wonder where we'd all be if we had Miss McGooghan's attitude, eh children?'

'Australia, Mr Spofforth,' said the children promptly.

'Australia...yes, very probably,' said Mr Spofforth, trying to decide if they were taking the mickey while Miss McGooghan mouthed 'Traitors' at them behind his back. 'So, who's going to take my suit to the cleaners? Any volunteers? What about you, Gail?' Gail had one of the Wise Men in a head lock, but she quickly let him go.

'Sorry, Boss,' she smirked. 'No can do. I'll be collecting the ticket money.' Miss McGooghan was about to say over her dead body, but the Headmaster got in first.

'Oh well done, Miss McGooghan,' he said sarcastically. 'What a brilliant idea! How wonderfully "*modern*"! Good on yer, cobber! Yes indeedy!'

Miss McGooghan gaped. For the first time in her life she was speechless.

'Are you serious, Boss?' said Gail, who had no sense of irony and could hardly believe her luck.

'No, of course I'm not serious,' said Mr Spofforth turning on her. 'If I catch you anywhere near the ticket money, Gail Fleshly, I shall velcro your bottom lip to the wallbars and use you for netball practice!' And he threw his Father Christmas costume at her. 'Back first thing on Friday, no starch in the trousers. Lawrence Kitten's charming mother will collect the ticket money, just like last year.' Lawrence put up his hand. Helen had particularly asked him to have a word about this.

'Excuse me, Mr Spofforth.'

'Yes, Lawrence, what is it?'

'Mum said to ask you, can someone else do the ticket money this year?' Mr Spofforth walked over with a puzzled look on his face as if the question had been in Japanese.

'Of course not,' he said. 'Out of the question!' and he clipped Lawrence cheerfully about the ear. 'Tradition, Lawrence, that's the thing! Carry on, Miss McGooghan...' And he left the room and could be heard humming 'God Rest Ye Merry' all the way back to his office.

After rehearsals, when Lambkin and Lawrence got to the cloakroom, Gail Fleshly was there ahead of them. She had crammed a boy called Marlon head first into one of the lockers and was pounding on the soles of his feet with a wooden mallet.

'Don't look at me! Don't look at me! Don't ever look at me!' she chanted as she bashed away. When she saw Lawrence she threw down the mallet and took him by the throat. 'Here, Florence the Kitten,' she said in a matey sort of way, 'how's your mum keeping these days? Must be a terrible worry for her, all that *ticket money* round the house.' Then she flicked Lawrence on the nose and let him go. 'You can't be too careful these days,' she whispered, 'there's a lot of very strange people about... Arf! Arf!' And she went off to her own locker, honking and snorting in the most alarming fashion.

'She's up to something,' said Lawrence rubbing his throat.

'No,' said Lambkin. 'She makes that noise when her brain cell divides.' Lambkin was putting Tina Marie carefully in her locker. She was in charge of the doll until after the nativity and knew that Kirsty would turn very ugly indeed if anything were to happen to it.

They got their coats and on the way out stopped to ask Marlon if he wanted his locker door closing. If they had just looked around the corner, into the next aisle, they would have seen something very interesting. Gail Fleshly had put on the Headmaster's Father Christmas costume and was busy cutting down her Arsenal scarf to make a beard. Lawrence was right, she was definitely up to something.

11
The Singing Red Midgets

Later that evening Lambkin was sitting in Helen's kitchen counting the school ticket money. Helen hated this job. Every year she dreaded it and could not remember how she had ever let Mr Spofforth talk her into it. Still, at least this year she had someone to help with the counting.

'I bet Roger and your gran are looking forward to seeing you in the nativity, aren't they?' Lambkin put down a big wad of notes and looked very seriously at Helen.

'Well to tell you the truth, Mrs Kitten...'

'She hasn't told them,' said Lawrence, coming in with a roll of cotton wool and some shoe polish for Joseph's beard.

'Haven't you, Lambkin?' said Helen. 'Why ever not?'

'It's just not worth it,' said Lambkin feeling guilty all over again. 'It would be okay if Dad came, and Man-in-the-Sack. But Gran hates Christmas. She'd probably shoot the innkeeper and mug the three Wise Men.'

'And Baby would very likely eat the donkey,' said Lawrence.

'Well I think you should tell them,' said Helen. 'Your gran is bound to feel differently when she knows you're playing Mary. Anyway, she can't hate

Christmas as much as I hate counting ticket money.' Helen looked accusingly at Lawrence. 'I thought you were supposed to get me off the hook.'

'Sorry, Mum, Mr Spofforth said you were a school tradition.'

'Great!' said Helen. 'Makes me feel like the nit nurse.' Just for a moment, as his mum was talking, Lawrence thought he saw something moving outside the kitchen window, something red, just for a second then it was gone.

'Come on, Mum,' he said, 'I thought you were going to help us look for costumes.' Helen sighed.

'I might as well,' she said, 'I've totally lost count. We'll look in the spare room.' She and Lambkin quickly scooped the ticket money into a big black cash box which they left on the kitchen table while they all went upstairs.

That was when the red 'something' that Lawrence had seen let itself in through the back door. It had Mr Spofforth's Father Christmas hood pulled right up and an Arsenal scarf covering most of its face, but it was still Gail Fleshly and she was busy doing what Gail did best, tucking other people's cash boxes under her arm and disappearing silently into the night.

At the very moment Gail was stealing the ticket money, Roger Bones was giving Man-in-the-Sack a list of the Christmas things they still had to get.

They had been at it for quite a while and had worked their way through most of the alphabet.

'R, S, T...T is for trampoline, tsetse fly and...turkey, of course, turkey! Now, how big? Do they weigh them with the giblets in or out, do you think?' Man-in-the-Sack shrugged and turned to Gran who had made a study of giblets and innards generally.

'Giblets in,' she said positively. 'Like babies. Baby weighs five-and-a-half stone, giblets in... They said so at the clinic...' But Roger was not listening, or rather he was not listening to *her*, for suddenly the sound of carols was drifting in on the night air.

'Ssh! Listen!' said Roger. 'The carol singers. Quick, Man-in-the-Sack, get the lights. Come on, Mother-in-Law.' He hauled Gran to her feet. 'Time for "God Rest Ye Merry".'

'Get off,' said Gran, 'I don't want a rest!'

'Then just come and be merry,' said Roger and was frog-marching her out when he noticed that someone had written 'Bog Off Vicar' in very large whitewashed letters on the living-room door.

This year the vicar had decided to dress the choir, and himself for that matter, as Father Christmases. There were thirteen of them, or at least there were *now*. Earlier, the vicar felt sure there had only been twelve, one big one, himself, and eleven small ones, the choir. Now suddenly there seemed to be eleven small ones, one big one and a middle-sized one who had brought her own collecting box.

'Don't dawdle, dear.' The vicar took the middle-sized one firmly by the arm as she tried to sidle off past the Boneses' house. 'Gather round the tree with the others.'

Gail Fleshly had no choice. The lights came on and she meekly shuffled over to the Pirates' Christmas tree while the vicar made a mental note to speak to his wife about the use of football scarves as beards.

When 'God Rest Ye Merry' ground to a halt, the vicar clapped his hands for silence.

'Beards on straight,' he said, scowling at a very small Father Christmas whose beard was on top of his head. 'Now, "Ding Dong Merrily" on a count of three…One, two…' But before he could get any further, Roger Bones appeared and took him cheerily to one side.

'Season's greetings, padre, I wonder if we might wait a moment for "Ding Dong Merrily"? You see it's my mother-in-law's favourite and she's just tidying up a few last minute Christmas greetings… You know how it is.'

'She won't be very long, will she?' asked the vicar. 'Only some of the younger ones have to be home by eight.'

'No, no,' said Roger. 'She's just gone for a fresh bucket… sorry *packet,* packet of Christmas cards.

She'll be out in a jiffy.' The vicar looked uncertain. 'I tell you what,' said Roger, 'while we're waiting, how about a little drop of something for the cold, eh?' He turned to the choir. 'Mince pies and ginger beer all round?' Eleven beards all nodded vigorously and one Arsenal scarf shook frantically from side to side. 'That's the stuff!' said Roger, winking at Man-in-the-Sack. 'And a nice nip o' grog for the padre! Christmas cheer, eh? That's what we want...'

But at that moment, the front door flew open and there stood Gran, whitewash all down her pinny and Betsy loaded to the spout with an interesting selection of Christmas baubles.

'You heard the man,' she shouted, wild-eyed at the sight of so many Santas. 'Christmas cheer! Start cheering, you non-existent little red midgets or you'll be wearing your bowels for bobble caps.' The vicar was horrified. Clearly the woman was deranged and the only thing for it was to play along.

'Hip, hip,' he said in a voice that got decidedly squeaky as the blunderbuss was shoved under his nose.

'Hooray!' shouted a terrified choir as Gran ran around tugging beards, apparently in the hope of finding a real one. Roger sighed. This was absolutely typical. Whenever they made some progress in the local community old Squitter-Head would do her best to spoil it.

Gail Fleshly, meanwhile, having met Lambkin's

granny before and with no intention of repeating the experience, scuttled off towards the gate while Gran, who had decided that the biggest Santa was the one to go for, was busy wrestling the vicar to the ground. Gail had edged round the struggling pair and would have made it too if Roger had not stepped in to pull Gran off the vicar.

'Sorry, padre,' said Roger, dusting the poor man down. 'Mother-in-Law's not very good at joined-up thinking.' He carefully removed Gran's hat. 'Mother-in-Law, have you ever been hit on the head with a collecting box at all?' Gran thought for a moment.

'You know,' she said, 'I don't believe I have.' Roger tapped Gail on the shoulder. 'May I?' he said and took the cash box before she could stop him. Then he went over to Gran, tilted her chin slightly to the left and brought the heavy box walloping down on top of her bonce as hard as he could. For a moment nothing happened then quite slowly Gran gave a little pirouette and crashed to the ground like a felled oak.

It really was a terrific performance. Man-in-the-Sack started clapping, even though he had seen it all before, and Gail found herself joining in.

'Hip, hip!' shouted the vicar.

'Hooray!' shouted the choir.

'Behold,' beamed Roger, 'I have smitten the Philistine for thee. This way, padre!' And handing

the cash box to the vicar, he led them all indoors.
Gail slowly stopped clapping and watched helplessly
as her ill-gotten gains disappeared inside the Pirates'
house, and Gran, stretched full-length on the
ground, was surprised to see a middle-sized Father
Christmas take off its Arsenal scarf and say, 'Bum!'
very loudly.

12
A Recipe for Disaster

Helen Kitten was sitting in the Pirates' living room and for once she did not mind counting the school ticket money. When she had discovered the cash box was missing she had almost fainted from the shock and now she was just happy to report that all the money was still there, every penny.

'But what was the vicar doing with it?' she asked.

'That's the odd thing,' said Roger, returning from the kitchen. 'The padre said he'd never seen it in his life before. Mince pie, anyone?' Helen and Lambkin both took one but Lawrence was too busy having one of his ideas.

'I don't think it's odd,' he said. 'I think it's highly suspicious and I think Gail Fleshly's got something to do with it.'

'Oh come on, Lawrence,' said Helen. 'I don't see how you can blame Gail for this.'

'He blames Gail for everything,' said Lambkin, with her mouth full. 'It's because she calls him Florence the Kitten.'

'Shut up!' said Lawrence and just then Helen let out a yell.

'Ow! I think I've broken a filling!' The next moment Lambkin did the same.

'Aargh! There's something in the mince pies...

Looks like, looks like pieces of lead shot.' And sure enough, Lambkin held up two small lead pellets.

'Good grief,' said Roger. 'That explains why the padre left in such a hurry and look at poor old Pustule.' Since eating a mince pie earlier, the macaw had evidently taken a funny turn, a downward turn you might say. In fact he was hanging bat-like and quite rigid beneath his perch. A scowl crept over Roger's face and he tore off the green paper hat he had been so pleased with when they had all pulled crackers. Suddenly he did not feel very festive. It had all been spoiled and as usual the reason was old Squitter-Head. 'Mother-in-Law, a word,' he shouted and stalked off to the kitchen.

Christmas for Gran meant the time of year when you boiled up your underwear, which she always did in her Special Stewpot and as Roger came in she was just ladling the carbolic.

'One thing,' he waved Helen's mince pie under her nose, 'one thing I ask you to do for our neighbours and you try to poison them! What did you put in them, eh? Out with it before I drown you in your own revolting…good grief, what *are* those?' He pointed at the pink and grey mess swirling in the pot but Gran was not about to be threatened in her own kitchen.

'Back off, Spittle Bucket,' she growled as the others arrived. 'There's nothing in those mincey pies I haven't used a thousand times before…'

'Go on, amaze me.' Gran had to think. The recipe had been in her family for years but had never actually been written down.

'Oil, suet, grease, the odd currant…' Her memory was not what it was.

'Flour?' suggested Helen helpfully.

'No,' said Gran.

'Mince meat?' Lambkin took a shot in the dark.

'No,' said Gran. 'Lard…' It was starting to come back to her. 'Oh, and the fatty bits from the side of the oven…' Roger looked puzzled.

'So nothing unusual there…' Helen could hardly believe her ears.

'Roger, that's disgusting! You didn't even bat an eyelid!' Gran turned on her.

'Here, who's been telling you about bats' eyelids? That's a Pirate secret, that is.' Roger gave Gran a shake.

'Look, there must be something you've forgotten. Come on, think, woman.' Gran struggled free and levelled her smalls' ladle at him.

'That's it, I've had enough of your accusations. Now get out of my kitchen before I hit you.' And before Roger could twitch a whisker, she whacked him as hard as she could. 'Quicker next time…' she grinned. Roger grabbed her by the throat and had begun to shake her properly when Lambkin found an interesting jar on Gran's chopping board.

'What's this?' She showed it to Roger who straightened out the faded label.

'Oh, just some mixed peel,' said Gran airily. 'Found it at the back of the poultice cupboard.' Roger held it under her nose.

'Look! Look, you dull-witted old albatross.' He was shaking Gran with one hand and the jar with the other. *'Pellets,* not peel! You've been feeding lead shot to everyone! Can't you read?'

Actually, Gran *could* read, if she wanted to, which until recently was more than you could say for Roger Bones.

'Oh, pardon me, Mr Huge-Brain McSmartbum,' she sneered. 'I forgot you were the world's reading expert. Well, I'm sorry, we can't all be scholars, can we?'

'Scholars? *Scholars!?'* His fingers tightened on her windpipe. 'This woman has the IQ of a coal scuttle!' Helen tried to prise him loose. 'She'd lose a battle of wits with a pile of natterjack toad droppings! I'm sorry, Helen, it's no use, we're going head to head on this one, it's time she confronted one of her victims...' He marched Gran into the living room and stood her in front of Pustule. 'There,' he said, hoping to stir some feelings of remorse, 'what do you say to that?' Pustule swung dismally beneath his perch.

'Doesn't matter what I say, he isn't going to answer, is he?' Gran cackled with glee at her own joke. Roger saw red. He wrenched Pustule from the perch and began to beat Gran about the ears with him.

'You hideous and unfeeling old woman!' he shouted through a cloud of feathers. 'Get up those stairs out of my sight and stay there till Boxing Day!'

'Charming!' said Gran but she knew she had overstepped the mark and she slunk off muttering, 'Whatever happened to peace and goodwill?'

'*Go!*' yelled Roger hurling Pustule after her. Gran dodged and caught the bird neatly in her ladle.

'Precious little of it round here!' she shouted and ducked out of the room quickly, before Roger could find a gun.

Roger slumped at the table and suddenly felt very sorry for himself.

'Honestly, Helen, why me? What have I done?'

'Oh, I shouldn't worry,' said Helen, 'it's her first Christmas ashore. It's probably all a bit strange.'

'Should suit her down to the ground,' said Roger, scraping together the last of the mince pies for Lambkin to give to Baby.

'You wait,' Helen went on, 'it'll all be different when she sees Lambkin in the school play.' Lambkin dropped the mince pies with a crash and Lawrence glared at his mum who was already going bright pink.

'Play?' said Roger. 'What play? Lambkin,

what play?'

'I'm sorry, Lambkin,' said Helen, 'I should have my mouth boarded up.' She turned to Roger and took a deep breath. 'Lambkin and Lawrence are in the school nativity and Lambkin hasn't told you because she thought, or to put it another way, she thought *Mrs Blood* might…'

'Keel haul the shepherds and take a cutlass to the Angel Gabriel?' Roger suggested.

'Something like that,' said Lambkin quietly, 'but look, Dad, I've been thinking it over. It doesn't matter. Gran can come if she wants.'

'Oh can she, indeed?' said Roger grimly. 'We'll see about that.'

Gran meanwhile was busy trying to revive Pustule. Not used to being upstairs, it took her a while to find the things she needed. The bird obviously needed oxygen. That bit was easy. She went into Spittle Bucket's room and threw open all the windows, letting in lots of nice cold air. Then she hung the macaw from the curtain rail using one of those jump leads most people keep in their garages and Roger kept in his wardrobe.

Next she raided Man-in-the-Sack's bunk where she found the small wind-up generator he used to get himself started in the mornings and she attached this to the other end of Pustule's lead. Finally she ran a second lead between the generator and the window frame, making a nice electrical circuit.

'There we are, my lad, we'll have you jumping about in no time,' she promised, but no sooner had she begun to wind the handle of the generator than she heard a noise in the garden below. It was the sort of noise someone makes when they are sneaking round outside your house with a big wooden ladder and trying very hard to make no noise at all. It is quite unmistakable.

Gran stuck her head out of the window and who should she see but Gail Fleshly, badly disguised as Father Christmas with an Arsenal scarf that had somehow got tangled up with her ladder.

'I thought I recognised that weaselly little mush when I was lying in the garden,' she said to herself. (Gran had once caught Gail Fleshly and her brothers trying to steal the Pirates' treasure and had even been put in charge of their Community Service until the social workers found she was giving them gunnery practice and put a stop to it.) Now she saw a chance to get back in Spittle Bucket's good books and have a bit of fun at the same time.

'Well, well, well,' she said loudly. 'It's not Christmas yet, is it?'

Gail stopped juggling with her ladder and froze to the spot. 'Oh bum,' she thought, 'Lambkin's grotty granny!'

'No, it's not Christmas,' said Gran very loudly, 'not by a long chalk. So if I was to find any imaginary red-faced old rogues a-creeping and a-skulking about my ship, I'd be entitled to give them a taste of their own medicine.'

What was she up to? Gail stared up at the window and saw Gran take a bottle from her coat.

'In fact,' Gran went on, 'I'd be entitled to give them a taste of *my* medicine...' Up close the liquid in the bottle looked like tar and the label said 'For Ye Damps and Squitters'. Gran took a big swig, rinsed it round her mouth and squirted it straight out of the window in a thick black stream.

She was shooting blind so not all of it hit Gail, but quite a lot of it did, enough to make Gail choke and drop the ladder very painfully on her foot.

'Urgh! 'Orrible it is,' said Gran, pretending not to hear the groans from below and re-corking her bottle. 'I'd rather have the damps and squitters any day.' And she waited patiently for Gail to stop retching. 'Ooh, it has gone quiet,' said Gran when it finally went quiet. 'You know, I think I'll go into another room, *in an entirely different part of the house*, and have a nice long sleep!'

When Gail heard this she wiped her face and gave a tarry little smile. Then, with much grunting and struggling, she got her ladder against the wall of the house and before you could say 'three years' probation' she was up at the window.

Sure enough the room was empty except for Pustule swinging sadly on the curtain rail. The bird

did not look capable of causing trouble but Gail gave him a vicious jab just to be sure and when he did not respond she decided it was safe to climb in. That was when she heard a noise.

It was the noise someone makes when they start up a power tool at the bottom of your ladder and do not give a hoot if you hear them. It is quite unmistakable.

Sure enough, there was Lambkin's granny at the foot of the ladder holding a whirring, whizzing chainsaw very nearly as big as herself. With her bright red hard-hat and matching ear-protectors, she cut a strange figure, and then quite deliberately she cut Gail's ladder.

'Oh bum!' said Gail lurching horribly and grabbing Pustule's jump lead by mistake. 'Oh bu...rrrghargh!' she said as five thousand volts went straight up her arm and sent her crashing down among the bits of chopped ladder in a small heap of shivered timber. As she lay twitching on the ground, with Gran chortling and cackling over her, her two least favourite words, 'Community' and 'Service', rang in her ears and gave her the strength somehow to get up and leg it across the front garden with Gran in hot pursuit.

The Pirates' front garden was not very big and most of it was taken up with the Christmas tree, around which Gail ran. After three or four laps she realised she had not seen Gran for a while, although she could still hear the noise of the chainsaw chopping into something. After a while that stopped too so Gail took the time casually to pick a splinter from her sleeve and even allowed herself a little smile.

'Old people,' she thought, 'no staying power.' Which might be true of the population at large, but not of Pirates. There was a nasty creaking sound, a cry of 'Timber!' and this old Pirate brought down five metres of Norwegian spruce, complete with fairy lights, squarely on Gail Fleshly's head.

13
Disgrace

Roger Bones had lined everyone up in the living room, all the Pirates plus Helen and Lawrence, just like Captain's Parade on board a ship at sea.

'Hands up all those who are going to the school Christmas play.' He walked slowly down the line and everyone he came to dutifully put up their hand, including the last person, who was wearing Gran's pinny but had the head and horns of a reindeer. Roger leaned closer until his nose was almost touching the red nose of the 'reindeer'.

'Not so fast, Mother-in-Law...'

'I am not Mother-in-Law,' said the 'reindeer', 'I am a jolly Christmas reindeer and I bring you a festive gift.' It was holding the top two metres of Roger's ruined Christmas tree, from which most of the needles had now fallen. The splintered end had been stuck in a bucket and Pustule had been parcel-taped to the top. As a finishing touch, two forty-watt light bulbs flashed gloomily among the branches. Roger's lip curled.

'I think we should all ask ourselves why Lambkin was afraid to tell us that she's appearing in her very first school play?' He looked the 'reindeer' in the eye. 'Did she suspect that one particular member of this household, I mention no names, might by her vile and Scrooge-like attitude, let the side down?

Might, in short, make her *ashamed* of her own family?' He had the 'reindeer' eyeball to eyeball. 'What do you think, mm?' The 'reindeer' had the good sense to remain silent. Roger looked at the miserable remains of his tree. 'And as for this...this travesty!'

'Listen, Spittle Bucket.' Gran pulled off the mask. 'I'm sorry about your tree but Creeping Fleshly was trying to break into the house. I had to do something.'

'What piffle! What poppycock! Don't make matters worse by telling Big Ones.' Roger liked his crew to take their punishment like men but Lambkin thought it was time someone spoke up for Gran.

'Just a minute, Dad, what about the cash box? What was it doing outside? Suppose someone *is* trying to steal the ticket money...' Lawrence nodded, hadn't he been saying as much all along?

'Someone like Gail Fleshly?' he suggested.

'Exactly!' said Gran. 'She was dressed like Father Christmas, so I sploshed her with my squitter-cure and whacked her with Spittle Bucket's tree.'

'She could just be telling the truth, Dad.'

'No she couldn't,' Roger snorted. 'I'm prepared to believe in Father Christmas, the Wizard of Oz or even the Tooth Fairy, but Mother-in-Law telling the truth? Hey, let's catch the fourteen bus to Real Street!'

'Even so,' said Helen, 'I think you should give her another chance, after all it is Christmas.' Now Gran hated the idea of a land-crab standing up for her but she swallowed her pride, smiled at Helen and nodded as hard as she could. Roger would not budge.

'Helen, have you heard the expression "Worse things happen at sea"?' He pointed at Gran. 'Well *this* is the worst thing that ever happened to me at sea and I don't intend to inflict it on others. Not at Christmas.' Gran clutched at her heart and began to faint.

'Aargh!'

'And you can stop that!' said Roger. 'Only people of goodwill and festive feelings should go to school Christmas plays. Naturally that rules Baby out, but I have decided that on this occasion you too, Mother-in-Law, must stay at home...' Gran let out a wail and began to sob. '...there to reflect upon the error of your ways as you huddle alone beside your bricked-up fireplace.' Gran buried her face in the tree.

'Noooooo!' she wailed.

'It's no use!' Roger folded his arms. 'My mind is made up!'

'Sorry, Gran,' said Lambkin quietly. Gran stopped weeping and opened one eye. She glared balefully at Roger, who was looking particularly pompous even for a Bones, and she realised the game was up.

'*Rats!*' she said and threw the tree at him before stomping out of the room to the sound of Baby's laughter.

At rehearsals in school on Friday, Lawrence kept a particular eye on Gail Fleshly. She had weird brown stains on her face, her arm was in a sling and she couldn't take her eyes off his cash box. Lawrence and Helen had both decided the money must go back to the school as soon as possible so he had brought it along to give to the Headmaster, only Mr Spofforth was far too busy to see him.

At the dress rehearsal that afternoon Lawrence could feel Gail's eyes burning into the box which, since he did not dare let it out of his sight, he had stuffed down the front of the dressing gown he was using as Joseph's tunic.

Miss McGooghan was getting more and more stressed out. There was still a whole day to go, but you could tell she just did not believe they would be ready in time. Lambkin made her entrance in Helen's blue bathroom curtains but Lawrence, who was supposed to be beside her, was busy looking for Gail and totally missed his cue.

'Okay,' said Miss McGooghan, 'you've just passed the sign that says "Welcome to Bethlehem!" You're going to get a room for the night! And here it is! The inn! It looks welcoming! Warm! Inviting!

You're full of hope! And...' She caught Lawrence three paces behind Lambkin, looking over his shoulder. 'Cut! Your wife's pregnant, Joseph! I think you might at least give her an arm to lean on you selfish toerag! Or is supporting the missus not *traditional* over here?'

At the mention of 'tradition' in came Mr Spofforth, carrying a very sorry looking Father Christmas suit.

'Gail Fleshly! Where is Gail?' he shouted, which was the question very much on Lawrence's mind.

'Here, Boss,' said Gail appearing from the back of the stage carrying a small angel.

'Just look at this.' The Headmaster waved the costume under her nose. 'Are you sure you took it to the cleaners?'

'Oh yes, Boss, definitely,' said Gail.

'But it's no different, if anything it's worse. And what's this down the front, smells like creosote?' Gail leaned forward to have a sniff and he clipped her soundly round the ear. 'Lawrence Kitten? Where's he?'

'Here, Sir,' said Lawrence lifting his beard.

'Ah, there you are. Have you got the ticket money?' 'Saved!' thought Lawrence pulling out the cash box.

'Yes, Sir, do you want it now?'

'No, no, no,' said Mr Spofforth. 'Far too busy, so are you. Bring it to my room tomorrow, before the

play. Thank you, Miss McGooghan, carry on...'
And he was gone, leaving Lawrence, cash box half
out of his dressing gown, staring straight into the
gap-toothed smile of Gail Fleshly.

'Did you see the way she was looking at this? I can't
leave it here, can I?' Lawrence and Lambkin were in
the cloakroom, putting their costumes away in their
lockers. For a moment Lambkin did not reply, then
she gave him Kirsty Trivet's doll, Tina Marie.

'Pull its head off.' Lawrence stared at her. 'Just do
it!' said Lambkin who already had the cash box
open and was rolling up the ticket money so it could
be pushed into the hollow body of the doll. After a
moment she realised someone was standing behind
her and she turned to find herself face to face with
Kirsty.

'Ah! Hello, Kirsty! Lawrence look, here's Kirsty!'
Fortunately Lawrence had his back to Kirsty.

'Can I have Tina Marie back until the concert?'

'*No!*' said Lambkin too loudly. 'I mean, not really,
if you don't mind. We need it for rehearsals.' Kirsty
was no fool. She could tell they were up to
something and tried to look past Lambkin to see
what Lawrence was doing.

'She's not an "it", she's a "she". Anyway, why do
you need her? You haven't even had the baby yet.' It
was fair comment. Lambkin had a large cushion up
her front and was obviously meant to be pregnant.

'Ah,' said Lambkin, pulling out the cushion and thinking quickly. 'Motivation... very important for actors.' Kirsty was much more interested in Lawrence.

'What's he doing? He's not being mean to Tina Marie, is he?'

'Not at all,' said Lambkin, flapping her arms to create a diversion. 'The nativity is all about bonding. He's bonding with the baby. Have you finished bonding yet, Lawrence?'

'Almost...' The doll's head clicked into place and Lawrence proudly showed it to Kirsty. Unfortunately the head was on backwards and Kirsty solemnly turned it round the right way.

'You're being mean to her, aren't you?'

'Certainly not,' said Lawrence. 'The nativity is all about caring.'

'She said it was about bonding.'

'And caring,' said Lawrence, giving Tina Marie a cuddle.

'Mmm, well you'd better not be mean to her, that's all, or I'll give you a good kicking.' And with that she marched off to her own locker.

As soon as she was out of sight, Lawrence and Lambkin tore off the doll's head and Lambkin began cramming the ticket money inside. Then they put back the head, put Tina Marie in Lambkin's locker and with a sigh of relief, turned the key.

Their hearts were beating so loudly, neither of

them heard a faint, tinny sort of banging coming from the far side of the locker room. This was caused by Kirsty Trivet's feet drumming gently against the side of a locker. Gail Fleshly had her firmly by the throat and was holding her at arm's-length while she spied on Lawrence and Lambkin.

14
Posh Folk

The following night was the night of the school Christmas play. Lambkin and Lawrence had to get there early, leaving Roger and Man-in-the-Sack still getting ready. Helen had promised to call for them on the dot of seven, which put them in a complete panic from four o'clock onwards.

As Roger had decreed, Gran was huddled in front of the bricked-up fireplace. She had a piece of sacking round her shoulders and was warming her hands on an old candle stub stuck to the back of the coal shovel. Nearby was Baby's pram and hanging perilously close, Roger's new evening suit, bought specially for the occasion. Baby was muttering quietly to himself and started to growl when he heard Roger's voice calling from the stairs.

'Mother-in-Law? Have you seen my new suit?' Without answering, Gran casually tossed the suit, plastic cover and all, into Baby's pram. There were a few horrible tearing noises and then a coat hanger flew out and pinged across the floor. Gran allowed herself a little smile.

'Didn't you hear me?' Roger came in wearing a shirt and tie but no trousers. 'My suit, I could have sworn I left it in here...' Baby made a very loud deliberate bottom noise in his direction. 'Oh dear,' said Roger, 'Daddy's little shipmate got a touch of wind?' He went across to the pram and leaned right over, his tie dangling in the very mouth of the hood. 'Is he going to be all right then, at home with his granny-wanny?'

Let's face it, it was never much of a conversation but that was as far as it got. The next instant Baby had him by the throat and was hauling him into the pram.

'Aargh! Mother-in-Law! Help me!' Gran did not look up, not even when Roger, who was about to disappear altogether, suddenly shot across the room as if he had been kicked in the pants and punched in the eye, both at the same time. 'Good grief! What's got into him?' His tie was like a piece of wet string and his lip was beginning to swell. Gran threw down her coal shovel with a clatter.

'He's upset, you insensitive great lugworm.'

'Upset? Why on earth is he upset?'

'Because, krill-wit, he wants to see his big sister in the school play.' The pram bobbed up and down and Baby made enthusiastic 'Yeah, yeah, yeah!' noises. Roger began hunting for his second-best trousers.

'Well I'm sorry, Mother-in-Law, it's just not on. Anyway, he wouldn't enjoy it.'

'Why not? Baby loves little children, don't you my treasure trove?' Baby gave a sinister chuckle.

'I know,' said Roger, 'spit-roasted in a light Cumberland sauce.' He shuddered at the memory.

'He stays at home and so do you.' Baby cleared his throat and spat a stream of suit buttons at Roger who luckily had stooped to pull his trousers on so they ricochetted harmlessly off the wall, at which point Baby said something very like 'Rats!'

'One thing's certain, Roger Bones,' said Gran. 'He's more of a Pirate than you'll ever be.' She was trying to light her pipe but suddenly her hands seemed too weak and trembly to hold the match. She let it fall to the hearth and coughed, painfully.

'What's the matter?' Roger knew he was a fool for asking.

'Nothing, I'm fine. Just a touch of my old trouble.' Gran dabbed her eyes with a corner of the sacking. 'Don't you worry about me. I'll be all right. You go off and enjoy yourself.'

'Thanks. I intend to.' Roger patted his hair.

'I can see the headlines now: "Home Alone Grandmother. Evil Son-in-Law gets fifteen years."' Gran began to sob.

'What are you talking about? You've got your mobile phone in case of emergencies.' Gran was not impressed.

'My only granddaughter's appearing in a play and I have to stay at home with a baby and a mobile phone. Anyway, I can't work it properly, I need someone to punch me buttons for me...'

'You tempt me strangely,' said Roger, and started towards her with his fist raised. Fortunately at that moment the doorbell rang. 'Good grief, there's Helen!' He found his jacket, mysteriously stuffed under the pillow in Gran's hammock, and struggled into it just as Man-in-the-Sack came in to show off his Christmas outfit.

He had been working on it all day and Roger had to admit it had been worth the effort. The theme was 'A Festive Yule Log'. He had wrapped himself in cardboard (still inside his sack of course) and had stuck on cotton wool snow, sprigs of holly and in the absence of a robin red-breast, he had managed to find a dead seagull and had made it a sort of bra out of red felt. The total effect was unusual but terribly seasonal.

'Bravo!' shouted Roger. 'We must show you to Helen. Cheerio, Mother-in-Law,' and they were gone without so much as a backward glance. No sooner had the door closed however than Gran leapt to her feet. If she and Baby were going to be home alone, at least they deserved a tot of rum for company, so using her coal shovel, she burst open the little cupboard where Spittle Bucket kept the visitors' grog.

'Aargh!' The cupboard was as cold and empty as his black heart. The swine had hidden it! Baby started to gnash his gums and snarl with rage but oddly enough Gran was not downhearted. This was because she had already been struck by *the* most wonderful idea. In fact so staggeringly warm and brilliant, so uniquely plush and squidgy was this idea that she just had to sit down and fan herself with the shovel, leaving Baby to howl and curse in the corner.

'Half a mo', my little sea urchin, don't you fret. What did old Spittle Bucket do when the singing dwarves came round, eh?' The noise from the pram dwindled to a low drooling as Baby thought about this and then grew to a gleeful giggle as he began to get her drift. 'That's right,' Gran smiled, 'he invited them in, didn't he? Yes! For a mincey pie and a nice nip o' grog...' She and Baby would go carol singing for drinks and snacks, nothing to it!

Before you could say 'Bog Off Santa', the two of them had taken to the streets and Gran was pushing the pram through one of those prosperous areas just made for a bit of land-based piracy. The streets had fragrant names like Juniper Close and Acacia Avenue, and the posh houses were called things like Camelot and Paddock's End.

'Grabalot and Pillock's End,' thought Gran as she stumped along. She was no socialist, far from it, but then again she had very little time for posh folk either. At last they stopped outside a large house called Mevagissey.

'Now this might well belong to a seafaring cove,' thought Gran, 'and one who's got a bit put by, I shouldn't wonder.' There was a nearly-new Volvo estate on the front drive and a tasteful holly wreath on the front door. 'Good for a nice tot of rum at any rate.' Baby started to get excited but Gran raised a warning finger. 'Come on now, my little bag o' bones, best behaviour.' And she pushed him up the drive to the front door.

Now it so happened that Mevagissey belonged to Gordon Spofforth, the children's Headmaster and his lady wife, Janice. They had no way of knowing Gran and she had no way of knowing them. All she saw was a rich looking house nicely decorated for Christmas, so she leaned hard on the bell.

Mr Spofforth was halfway through shaving when he opened the door to a frightful old woman with a wretched child in a pram and her grubby finger stuck to his bell. He lifted the finger off, wiped his glasses on the shaving towel and looked her up and down.

'Yes, what is it?'

'Evening, Cap'n,' said Gran, 'compliments of the season...' The child's pram was crudely decorated and the old woman had hung bottle corks on strips of tinsel from the brim of her hat, giving her the appearance of a festive Crocodile Dundee. She was clearly a beggar of some sort but Mr Spofforth was already late for the school play and now was not the time.

'Come along, I'm in rather a hurry. What exactly do you want?' This took Gran by surprise, surely it was obvious?

'We're carol singers, Cap'n...' and to prove it she ripped into 'We Wish You a Merry Christmas' very loudly but with no noticeable tune.

'Here, stop that! Stop that. Do you hear me? Just stop that!' Gran did as she was told. Mr Spofforth had spent his life getting small people to do what he told them and he was more than a match for some old boiler singing drunken songs.

'Now you listen very carefully,' he said, 'I think the thing for you to do is to get that poor child indoors, do you see? As quickly and quietly as you possibly can. So off you go. Good night to you.' With that he began to close the door but Gran was ready for this and quickly got her foot in the way.

'Here what about my mincey-pie?'

'Your "mincey-pie"?'

'And my nip o' grog, that's right. And don't you worry about Baby, he'll have some of mine.'

'Madam.' Spofforth looked down his long thin nose at her. 'I should say you'd had quite enough to drink for one night. Now kindly remove your foot.' And with that the door shut firmly in her face. Baby sniggered and Gran could only resort to shouting abuse through the letterbox.

'And a Merry Christmas to you too, you miserable squint-eyed la...' The door flew open and Spofforth stood glaring down at her. 'La, la, la, la, la, la laah ...' Gran did her best to turn it into 'We

Wish You a Merry Christmas', but without the benefit of a tune it fooled no one. The Headmaster leaned over and looked her in the eye.

'If you are not down that drive and off my property in precisely ten seconds, I shall fetch a policeman to you. Is that quite clear?'

'As the crystal stream, Cap'n. As the crystal stream.' Gran gave a little curtsy and scurried back to the pram. 'And a Happy New Year to you and yours.'

Gran struggled off towards the street with Mr Spofforth watching her all the way. The day had started badly thanks in the main to Gail Fleshly. He had spent hours cleaning his own costume himself and had not even begun the process of gluing on his Father Christmas beard, the bit he enjoyed best. Now that old woman had made matters worse. He had about ten minutes to get changed when he normally allowed himself at least an hour. He went inside cursing the homeless and determined to make Gail Fleshly suffer.

Gran meanwhile had already set her sights on another house. This one was called Broad Acres, which she thought had a nice generous ring to it. She leaned on the bell and hammered the knocker a few times for good measure. The person who answered wore a turban and a long robe. 'Foreign royalty,' she thought. 'We've cracked it!'

'Evening, Cap'n...' The person removed the turban and began drying her hair which was still wet from the shower. 'Oh, beggin' your pardon, ma'am...' (What was the matter with these posh folk, they seemed to spend all their time in the bathroom.) 'I couldn't trouble you for a mincey pie, could I?'

'Sponging old ratbag!' said the posh woman. 'Get a job!' And immediately slammed the door. Baby laughed out loud. None of this was going the way Gran had pictured it.

'I suppose a tot o' rum's out of the question?' she yelled through the closed door. Over the noise of running water, they could just hear the woman shout, 'Clear orf, parasite!'

Baby started swearing quietly to himself.

'I know, I know, posh folk, eh?' said Gran. 'You can see why people beat them senseless with rolled up newspapers.' And she pushed the big black pram out into the street and trudged off past all the swanky houses with their twinkling Christmas lights.

A few minutes later Mr Spofforth came out of his house in a state of total confusion. The bottoms of his Father Christmas trousers seemed to be full of pine needles which had worked their way down inside his red wellingtons. He was so hot and bothered that the spirit gum on his beard had lost its 'stick' and to cap it all, Janice, who was doing nothing more useful than watching 'Coronation Street' had the nerve to ask if he knew he was late.

'Yes, thank you, Janice,' he shouted. 'I'm late now and I shall be late back, so don't wait up!' And he slammed the front door and got into his Volvo, sticking down his beard as best he could on the way.

Seconds later, he was crossing Acacia Avenue when who should appear out of the shadows but the old woman with the pram. She was muttering to the child and was obviously quite unhinged. 'Someone should take them off the streets, at least over Christmas.' Mr Spofforth had just had this generous thought when, without warning, the old bat swung the pram right out in front of him and walked straight under the Volvo's wheels.

Actually Gran had seen another likely looking house and had decided to give it one last go before calling it a night. The next thing she remembered was a blinding light, a crash, a weightless floaty sort of feeling and then the cold wet hardness of the road pressed against her face. 'Baby!' she thought. 'My poor little sea urchin!' But in fact the pram had rolled safely to a halt on the far side of the road. Gran felt strange, sort of cold and numb and now there were these red boots, and hands turning her over and...

'Aargh! No, not you, go away!' It was the non-existent old rogue himself, leaning over her and polishing his glasses if you please. 'Get away from me, get away! You don't exist!' she groaned and then everything went dark.

15
A Christmas Miracle

When Gran came to her senses she found herself safely in her chair at home but there was something sharp, tap-tap-tapping on her cheek.

'Get off, get away from me!' she shouted, fearing the old rogue's bony finger. Then her eyes uncrossed and poor old Pustule swam into view. He was still taped to the top of the tree which had fallen against her chair so that his beak was about a centimetre from her nose. 'Oh, it's you!' She closed her eyes. 'I had this terrible dream. I dreamt I was knocked down in the street and the driver of the car was...' She opened her eyes to see Father Christmas coming out of the kitchen carrying a mug of tea. 'Aargh! It's you! Get away, you Red Devil! You don't exist!' She crossed all her fingers to ward off the evil eye.

'Ah good,' said Mr Spofforth, 'you're awake. Feeling a bit better?' He tried to give her the tea but Gran just gaped at him and made weak flapping motions. The Headmaster really was most fearfully late but at least he had used his time in the kitchen to get his beard properly stuck down. 'You've had a nasty shock,' he said. 'Mind you, come to think of it so have I...' He took a big swig of tea himself and wondered whether just to leave the old bag and risk the law suit. Then he caught sight of Pustule bobbing mournfully on the tree. 'What's the matter with him?'

'Something he ate,' muttered Gran, finding her voice at last. With surprising gentleness Mr Spofforth eased Pustule off the tree and peered inside his open beak. Then he grasped the macaw firmly by the feet and whacked him hard on the back of the head. There was the pinging sound you hear in westerns when bullets ricochet round the saloon, then Pustule coughed hoarsely and opened one watery eye.

'Hey, Doc,' he croaked, 'take my advice, steer clear of the mince pies.' Mr Spofforth returned him carefully to his perch but when he turned back to Gran he almost fell flat on his face. The old woman had crawled over and was kneeling on the floor right behind him, hugging him round the legs.

'Oh, thank you, Father Christmas, thank you!' She yanked down hard on his beard and Spofforth let out a yell. This was enough, Gran was totally convinced. 'I believe! I believe! I take it all back! You *are* real! It's a Christmas miracle!'

'No, no, dear lady, calm down!' This was all he needed, the old trout had gone completely doo-lally. 'Something stuck in the bird's throat, that's all. Really it was nothing…'

'Hey, to you maybe…' squawked Pustule as the Headmaster struggled to get Gran to her feet.

'Look, you're obviously much better.' He

managed to loosen her fingers from his belt. 'And I really must fly. There are a lot of children depending on me...' Gran straightened up at once and tapped the side of her nose.

''Course there are, Father Christmas, 'course there are. Only right and proper...'

'No, no, you don't understand.' He was trying to be patient. 'I have to be at the school.'

'The school!' Gran's eyes lit up at once and in the corner, Baby's pram began to bob up and down excitedly. 'Oh, please Your Santaship, take us with you!' Spofforth was horrified.

'What!'

'Well, you can't leave us here.' A crafty look crossed Gran's face. 'I mean, no offence, Your Seasonalness, but it was you knocked me over. There could be complications...' And to prove it she had a sudden 'dizzy spell'. The Headmaster managed to catch her and realised that he did not have time to argue.

'Oh very well, but we must be quick!'

'Aye, aye, Cap'n!' She went over to the pram rubbing her hands. 'Come on, Baby, you heard His Festiveness. Looks like it's Christmas after all!'

Meanwhile, over at the school, Lambkin, Lawrence and Miss McGooghan were in the cloakroom along with three wise men, four shepherds, seven angels, Kirsty Trivet and the whole of the third year recorder group. The one person who was *not* there was Mr Spofforth and Miss McGooghan was at her wits' end.

'Where is he?'

'Chicken pox, Miss?' suggested one of the wise men.

'Don't be wise, Alan.' Miss McGooghan was not in the mood. 'I need this like I need a giraffe. Look, it's no good, we'll just have to start without him.'

'You can't, Miss,' said Kirsty Trivet, 'it's not traditional.'

'Oh can't I? You watch me, kiddo. Right, line up everybody, recorders to the front. Lawrence, Lambkin, where's Tina Marie?' Lambkin went to her locker and opened the door. Horror! Panic! It was empty.

'She's gone, Miss!'

'Gone?' Lawrence pushed past hoping there might be some mistake but there was no mistake. It was a very small locker and it was very, very empty. 'She's gone!' said Lawrence. In the horrible silence that followed, Kirsty Trivet walked up to him.

'Gone *where?*' she asked and kicked him very hard in the leg.

Even before Lawrence hit the ground, Tina Marie was slipping quietly out of the back door and into the playground, stuffed down the front of Gail Fleshly's biker jacket. Gail was preparing to leg it into the night when she saw something that froze the gap-toothed smile on her weaselly little mush. A pram, decorated for Christmas, appeared to be floating along the top of the playground wall. She was still trying to puzzle this out a moment later when the Headmaster's Volvo swung through the school gates with Baby's pram bungeed to the roof-rack.

Now this called for some quick thinking which was not Gail's best thing and she was still doing medium-paced thinking when the Headmaster spotted her and wound down his window.

'Gail Fleshly! You are in deep, deep doo-doo. Oh dear me, yes! Deep and dreadful...' Gran was sitting next to His Prominence and this outburst surprised her. She was surprised that he knew individual children by name, and even more surprised that he knew words like 'doo-doo'. However, she was not half so surprised as Gail, who reckoned the Boss must be psychic to have found out about the ticket money so quickly. That was when the Virgin Mary appeared in the doorway with Joseph limping along behind.

'Quick!' shouted Lambkin. 'Stop her! She's stolen the ticket money!' The Headmaster only wanted to talk about his trousers but when he heard this he threw the Volvo into gear and roared off in pursuit of Gail who was heading for the far side of the playground with the clear intention of climbing the wall. Gran liked nothing better than a good chase, particularly in a car like the Volvo which she felt blended safety and performance in a very acceptable way. She quickly got into the spirit of it and began to shout encouragement.

'Run her down! Flatten her! Drive right over her!' In the heat of the moment she even found herself grabbing hold of His Noëlness's knee but quickly remembered her manners.

Gail meanwhile had come to a halt in the corner of the yard, forcing the Headmaster to pull up a few metres away. As the car stopped there was a loud twanging noise and a moment later Baby's pram, trailing its bungees, came rolling down the windscreen and off across the bonnet.

'Good grief!' said Spofforth. 'I'm not insured for any of this!'

'Don't you worry, Your Bank Holidayship, you've done your bit. You just leave it to Baby...Go get her, Baby!' Gran screamed out of the window. 'Tear out her toe-nails and use them for toothpicks!'

The great black pram trundled slowly to the ground and rolled towards Gail. At first she was more curious than frightened. She stood there with Tina Marie half in, half out of her jacket and stared at the pram which had begun to shudder and give off a strange green light. The light grew brighter and brighter, and then clouds of smoke came billowing from the hood.

'This is for your benefit, Your Snowy-Whiteness,' said Gran proudly, 'he doesn't normally put on a show like this.' Spofforth gulped and hid his eyes.

Bathed in the green light from the pram, Gail was now well and truly scared and in her panic could only think of throwing Tina Marie as far as possible over the playground wall. She threw the doll as hard as she could, high up in the air, but Baby, who liked a challenge, chuckled grimly and the barrels of two flintlock pistols appeared in the mouth of the pram.

It was a difficult shot at best, but in a pitch black playground what happened next was nothing short of amazing. 'Kaboom!' Both pistols went off together with a deafening roar. Tina Marie's head flew one way, her arms and legs flew the other and her body disappeared in a cloud of smoke in the middle. The echo of the pistol shots rolled round the empty playground and then suddenly it was raining money, banknotes fluttering down out of the sky.

'*Yes!*' said Lawrence and Lambkin, still watching from the school doorway, and they did high-fives to celebrate. But Baby was not quite finished. Gail made the mistake of trying to collect the falling money and cram it into her pockets. The pram let out a howl of rage and, tyres smoking, Baby charged at Gail knocking all the breath from her body and leaving her pinned to the playground wall.

'What a show-off!' said Gran indulgently and patted Father Christmas on the arm.

ride in it.' Roger tried to land a punch but could not get past Mr Spofforth.

'I am sorry, Headmaster.' He turned and mouthed furiously at Gran. 'Mother-in-Law, do you ever think before you open your mouth?' Gran thought for a moment.

'No.'

That was it. Roger was determined to strangle her, quite sure that no court in the land would convict him. Lambkin spoke up.

'Calm down, Dad. Mr Spofforth's right. Without Gran and Baby, Gail would have got away with the ticket money. You see, Gran must have been telling the truth all the time.'

'Oh I was,' said Gran, 'some of the time.'

'She's a credit to you all, Mr Bones!' said the Headmaster, giving Gail's ear a vicious tweak. Lambkin took Roger's hands from Gran's throat and held them in her own.

'Come on, Dad. Give her a big hug.'

'Give her a big *what?*' Roger stepped back like a man scalded. Was the girl mad? It was Man-in-the-Sack who came forward to make the first move. Looking very dignified in his yule log costume, he took Roger on one side and Gran on the other, and hugged them both.

'Bravo!' said Mr Spofforth. Everyone cheered and soon Lambkin was hugging Man-in-the-Sack, he was hugging Helen, Mr Spofforth was hugging

everybody, and who knows, somewhere in the scrum, by accident of course, perhaps even Roger hugged his mother-in-law.

Miss McGooghan hated to spoil a party, but somewhere along the line she remembered they still had a nativity play to perform.

'And we've got a problem, Chiefy. Look at this.' She showed the Headmaster some scorched bits of Tina Marie. 'What are we going to do?' (Kirsty Trivet knew exactly what *she* was going to do, season of goodwill or not she attacked Lawrence with a shepherd's crook.)

'Dear, oh dear,' said the Headmaster, 'this is terrible! We can't have a nativity without a baby. It's not traditional. What can we do?'

'Don't you worry about a thing, Your Yuletideness,' said Gran, stepping forward. 'I think I may have the answer,' and she turned to the big black pram which was already shuddering with glee. 'Come along, my little sea slug, it's *showtime!*'

For a long moment everyone froze and then the Pirates' cry rang down the length of the school corridors.

'NOOOOOO!'